'California or bust!'

For Leah Cabot, gen... surviving member of h... ...ges of the American Civil War, the trek Westward starts as a journey towards a dream.

But the dream turns quickly into a nightmare.

Extremes of heat and cold, thirst and starvation, savage Indians and renegades all take their toll on the toiling group of pioneers. And overriding everything for Leah is the cynical contempt of Cole McCullough, the enigmatic stranger who mysteriously joins their wagon train. How can Leah, a loyal daughter of the North, feel anything but loathing for this Southerner—an enemy in their midst?

Wild Rivers Run

Robyn Stuart

MILLS & BOON LIMITED
London · Sydney · Toronto

First published in Great Britain 1983
by Mills & Boon Limited, 15–16 Brook's Mews,
London W1A 1DR

© Robyn Stuart 1983
Australian copyright 1983
Philippine copyright 1983

ISBN 0 263 74190 7

04/0283

Set in 10 on 10½pt Linotron Times

Photoset by Rowland Phototypesetting Ltd
Bury St Edmunds, Suffolk
Made and printed in Great Britain by
Cox and Wyman Ltd, Reading

CHAPTER ONE

LEAH drew aside the puckered canvas cover and, balancing one foot on the wagon tongue, eased herself to the ground. The camp had settled now, the only sound the faint stirring of the wind in the cottonwoods. She took a few steps into the night stillness.

The sky was studded with stars—more stars than she remembered from back East—but the moon outshone even their number. Leah took a breath and shut her eyes.

She could smell the water, smell the free flowing water that bubbled up from the underground spring, the first clear water they'd come to in weeks. Tomorrow morning, she promised herself, she'd feel that water on her skin, pure and sweet and cool . . .

Leah stiffened at the footfall behind her, a dark shape rising suddenly out of the brush to her right. Too late a scream rose to her lips as a hand was clamped quickly over her mouth. In the pale, sharp moonlight, she saw the naked blade of a knife glittering inches from her throat.

'Bring me what I ask—stay quiet—and no harm will come to you.' The voice was low and raw and desperate. 'Do you understand?'

Half dazed in fear, Leah managed a bare nod.

'All right then.' The hand dropped from her lips. 'Turn around and I'll tell you what I need.'

Slender body swaying lightly, head down, Leah moved to obey the man, and as she turned, she heard him draw a rasping breath. Abruptly his voice came again from the darkness.

'Look at me.'

Slowly Leah lifted her chin, the heavy curtain of her hair parting, the silvered moonlight falling full on her cameo clear face. White to the lips, she looked across the glistening blade to the man who held it.

With the impact of a blow his physical strength struck at her.

He was of no more than medium height, but a sense of terrible, leashed force clung to his muscular body, to his disturbingly wide shoulders, to his heavy arms. His buckskin breeches were stained with dirt, strained taut over hard thighs, and through the laces of his belted, buckskin shirt, Leah caught a glimpse of a brown chest, matted with thick, dark hair. A stetson was slanted low over his forehead, the ends of his brown hair curling long over his collar. His face was sun blistered, wind seared, streaked with grit, half hidden by a tangle of dark beard and moustache—yet Leah could still discern the almost wolfish cast of gaunt cheeks and prominent, ridged cheekbones.

Beneath straight, black brows, his eyes gleamed cat yellow—and they were the hunted eyes of an animal. Fiercely they searched her face.

And in the haunted depths of that gaze, Leah saw a pain so deep her fear was forgotten before a compassion that tore at her heart. Her own eyes softened, the tender, tip-tilted curve of her lips parting.

In the star-dusted shadows their glances held for a brief eternity.

Then, deliberately, he let his eyes travel to the slim, moon-dappled line of her throat, down the silhouette of her body, lying lithe and supple beneath her shift. Without touching her, he seared her flesh—something so hot and vital in those tawny eyes, she felt branded for all time.

With a swift, unexpected movement, he reached one hand to the cascade of her hair, letting the strands fall through his fingers. His caress strayed to the curve of her cheek, his gentleness oddly at variance with his looming power—and more devastating than violence. Leah felt her body quicken. Felt it tuned to a bewildering pitch—ready to sing a melody she had not yet learned, or only dimly imagined.

Abruptly the hand against her cheek began to tremble—the hand that gripped the knife going rigid. The blade slipped to the ground. As if it had shook through her own body, Leah felt the man's convulsive shudder. He crumpled forward, slumping first to his knees before falling heavily, face down.

Leah stared at the still figure, uncomprehending. The wondering array of so many emotions had left her numb. She took a faltering step backward, arms straight at her sides. At the shrill bark of a dog, she started, sucking in a ragged breath.

The noise jarred her from her stupor. Quickly she moved again to the wagon. The water bucket was fastened at the back, near one of the heavy, iron-rimmed wheels, and only inches above Birdie Gordon's head. As Leah gripped it, Birdie gave a heavy snort and flopped over.

Fingertips poised on the handle, Leah held motion-less—but there was only silence. Satisfied that Birdie was still sleeping, she lifted the bucket down, reaching also for the towel that was flung over the tail gate, and returned to kneel at the man's side.

With gentle hands, Leah turned him over. Taking the dipper from the bucket, she tilted it to his lips and he sucked greedily at the liquid. She moistened the towel, and as she touched it lightly to the ridged bruise at his temple, he moaned softly. Slowly his eyes opened.

Leah's heart checked and began to beat again. She bent close, wiping his face as he watched her, and the heaviness of her hair fell like a veil over them both.

'I—I thought I'd dreamt you—'

As if the intensity in his voice, in his eyes, held a terror greater than the point of his knife, Leah drew sharply back, her hand striking the dipper as she moved, sending it clattering noisily against the bucket.

'What in tarnation—'

Birdie Gordon rolled from under the wagon bed in a half crouch. 'Leah, child! Are you all right?' Her voice filled the night stillness as she prodded the wagon cover with the tip of her rifle. 'Leah?'

Leah swallowed and found her voice. 'I'm over here, Birdie!'

Winchester cradled in the crook of one arm, Birdie came close. The sharp eyes in the blunt face took in Leah and the man, and she scratched at the spikes of grey hair poking up randomly from her head. 'Where in the devil did *he* spring from?'

'What's the trouble here, ladies?'

Bristling, Birdie turned on the wagonmaster, his bulky figure looming up dark against the moonlight.

'Watch your language, Alonzo Simms! I never laid claim to being a lady and I never will!' She sniffed. 'And I was just about to find out what the trouble was when you came bargin' up like a whole herd of gun-shy buffalo!'

Simms gave his steeple crowned sombrero a jab. 'Birdie Gordon, you are the doggonedest woman! I reckon I better talk to Miss Leah if I want to get anyplace.' He shifted his considerable girth from one foot to the other, bobbing his heavy head towards the stranger. 'What's going on here? I was on night watch when I heard the ruckus.'

'I—I couldn't sleep so I left the wagon and—'

Leah halted. She looked down. The stranger's eyes, narrowed now to gleaming slits, still watched her—and they held neither fear nor entreaty. He was entrapped but unafraid.

Only she knew he was conscious—only she knew the truth . . .

'You left the wagon—' Alonzo Simms prompted.

She should tell them—all the years of her life urged her to tell them the truth—and she knew, as she'd known nothing else in that life, that she would not tell them.

'I left the wagon and found him lying here,' Leah finished steadily. 'He's hurt—a blow to the head.'

'Is he armed?'

From the corner of her eye, Leah caught the gleam of the knife, lying half hidden and forgotten in the grass. She slid one hand carefully behind her, covering the blade, and lifted a level gaze to Simms. 'No, he isn't armed—see, his holster's empty.'

Alonzo Simms ran a hand over his heavy jaw. 'Could be he was bushwhacked.'

'And could be he's a bushwhacker!'

Birdie was eyeing the stranger speculatively. She prodded his still figure with the toe of one boot, but there was no response. 'Well, whoever—or whatever—he is, it don't seem likely he'll give us much trouble tonight.' She nodded to Simms. 'Tote him closer to the wagon, where I can keep an eye on him. Maybe by mornin' he can give us some answers.'

Effortlessly Alonzo Simms slid an arm under the man's middle and hoisted him up, but as the wagon-master straightened—the stranger draped head down over one shoulder—he jabbed again at the sombrero. 'Sure you'll be all right?'

'Righter than Missouri rain!' Birdie patted the barrel of her Winchester for emphasis and then jerked a thumb at the big man. 'Just do as I say and quit your jawin'.'

Simms set the man down near the wagon and, muttering, lumbered away again into the night.

'If that isn't the doggonedest woman!'

Coming slowly to her feet, Leah brushed away the dirt and bits of dusty grass that clung to her shift. Her eyes lingered on the stranger's still form.

'Child—' The sharpness of Birdie's voice drew Leah's gaze. 'Are you tellin' me the truth about what happened out here? You got a mighty strange look on your face.'

'I'm fine—you mustn't worry about me. Goodnight, Birdie.'

Leah climbed quickly into the wagon bed. What had happened to her in the quiet darkness of this prairie night?

She'd lied for a man. Leah Cabot had lied for a criminal who very probably had meant to rob them all.

Leah Cabot had stared duty in the face and for the first time in her life—chosen the opposite path.

And in the hollow of her hand lay the naked blade of a stranger's knife, sharp to the touch—and yet strangely like a caress.

Duty, to Leah Cabot, had always meant Cabot Academy. And Grandfather John.

'There has been a Cabot Academy in Boston since there was a Boston,' Grandfather John was fond of saying in every commencement address. 'It was Jeremiah Cabot, my great-grandfather, who founded this school in 1631.'

When Leah was a child she'd thought Grandfather John, with his flowing beard and fierce eyes, was an old Testament patriarch—like Abraham or Isaac. When she grew older, she realised he thought of himself in the same way. He was the patriarch of Cabot Academy and the guardian of its dream.

'It was Jeremiah Cabot's dream to create a place of learning where all would be welcome,' Grandfather John would tell the graduates every Spring, 'rich and poor alike! Where the love of learning alone would matter—not money or position or name.'

Save one name, Leah always thought silently. Cabot. For it was part and parcel of Cabot Academy's tradition—Jeremiah Cabot's dream—that it was always a Cabot who headed the school, a Cabot who set its rules and made its regulations. Jeremiah Cabot had begun the school and the traditions and the dream—and he'd passed all three down to succeeding generations, the line continuing unbroken to Grandfather John.

But fate, in the guise of a virulent diphtheria

epidemic, intervened in the dream. It robbed the Academy of its heir apparent, Grandfather John of his son, Leah of both her parents.

Yet there was still Micah.

'We must make a pledge, Leah, a pledge that we will never forget our Mother and Father,' Micah had declared solemnly that day after the funeral, the day they'd come to live with Grandfather John. 'Pledge, Leah!'

And dutifully Leah had given her word.

But the memories of a five-year-old girl and a seven-year-old boy blur easily, and soon it seemed life had always been lived in the small, dark house adjacent to the Academy.

Micah flourished in the sombre atmosphere, growing to be a studious, serious-eyed boy—and as much like Grandfather John as John Cabot could make him.

Leah, too, had been faithful to the dream, indeed she had no time for dreams of her own. Her days and years were filled with baking and mending and cleaning, lessons in the evening with Grandfather John, obligations to the Academy. And had she had the time, she'd wondered only occasionally, would she have been allowed to dream?

But again fate intervened in Jeremiah Cabot's legacy. Only this time it wore the grisly mask of Civil War, and the strife that ripped a nation in two changed their lives as well. Forever.

First it took Micah.

'There's been a battle,' Grandfather John had told Leah that warm afternoon in July, 'in a little town in Pennsylvania—Gettysburg.'

She'd come in from marketing to find him, as always,

in his worn leather chair, the paper, as always, in his lap.

Everything was as always—except his voice. That had become a stranger's voice.

The paper slipped to the floor and Leah lifted it, knowing even before she read the casualty lists the name she would find there.

'Lieutenant Micah Cabot.' And now her voice was a stranger's voice, too.

The Academy was taken next.

Larger schools—wealthier schools with wealthier alumni—were able to weather the war-inflicted cutbacks, the hardships. But Cabot Academy's only resources were its people—and those went swiftly.

They lost the older students and the younger members of the faculty first. Grandfather John went to the depot to see them off, Leah following in his wake, and all around them the air was frantic with farewells and women's tears—and the eagerness of young men to get to war.

'We'll be back by Christmas!' they'd shouted as the troop train pulled out of the station, and John Cabot shook his head.

'Why do men always say they'll be back from war by Christmas? They never are, they never will be.'

Those first men watered with their blood the Virginia countryside and the hills of Georgia. And then the younger men came, to take their brother's place or their father's place—on the field and in the cemeteries, where rows of white crosses marked the end of dreams.

But fate had not quite taken all of the Cabot dream, not yet.

'We're going to California,' Grandfather John had told Leah quietly, one winter evening in 1864. 'I'm going to start a school there—and you're going to help me.'

Needle poised in one hand, mending on her lap, Leah had said nothing. There was nothing to say. Her life had been made up of duties done and orders obeyed. This was but one more.

Grandfather John stood at the mantel, back to the fire, and his eyes did not see her—nor even the room he'd lived almost a lifetime in. They saw a new land and a new school—and an old dream.

'People say California is a golden land! Why, it has mountains and rivers—and it's new! New, like the East was when Jeremiah Cabot first came. And so many people will be going there! Oh, not right now, because of the war, but later they'll come by the thousands! People who'll need schools!'

With the first sign of Spring, Grandfather John had started off, as eager and as impatient as a boy—as perhaps Jeremiah Cabot had been all those years ago. He'd brushed aside all Leah's concerns for his safety. True, he was a schoolmaster, not a frontiersman, but he had a willing spirit, and a dream. He could learn all he needed to know.

He would take a steamboat as far as Independence, Missouri, and then join one of the small fur-trading caravans heading for Fort Laramie.

Fort Laramie, Wyoming Territory, stood as the last outpost of civilization on the very edge of the American wilderness. It was five hundred miles out of Missouri, and the central meeting place for trappers and traders and prospectors—anyone who'd been or was going to the new land beyond the mountains. Here Grandfather John would gather information and make plans and wait for Leah.

The swell of settlers heading for California and Oregon had tapered off to a trickle during the last years of the war. Union soldiers were too busy killing their brothers to handle the Indians, and without their protection, travel West had become too dangerous for all but the hardiest. Yet the war couldn't last forever—why, even now US Grant had Lee and his Johnny Rebs on the run! And after the war—

'After the war,' Grandfather John had told Leah, 'you'll join me at Fort Laramie and together we'll go to California.' He'd gripped her shoulders, and his hands had dug into her flesh, as if by his very will he could infuse her body with his dream. 'The Promised Land, Leah, that's what people call California! The Promised Land—that's where we'll build Cabot Academy anew!'

On April 9th, at Appomattox Courthouse, General Robert E. Lee and his Army of Northern Virginia surrendered to Ulysses S. Grant. The end had come for the South.

'But for me,' Leah had said aloud into the stillness of the lonely house, 'it means neither an end nor a beginning. It will be the same life in California, lived in the same way, for the same dream. Their dream.' And then she'd busied herself quickly—thrusting away the brief bitter thought that had echoed so ominously in the silence.

She sold the house, as she'd been instructed, the furnishings—the possessions of four generations of Cabots—and as Grandfather John had done, booked passage to Independence, Missouri, premier 'jumping off' place for the way West. Once there, she looked for Alonzo Simms.

'Mr Alonzo Simms,' Grandfather John had written

her shortly after the surrender, 'is a wagonmaster of excellent repute, and already he is preparing to organise his first caravan West since the war. Secure a place on his wagon train.'

Leah tracked Alonzo Simms down in an outfitters shop, seeing to provisions for the trip. The noise, inside and out, was terrific, a frantic medley of jingling harnesses, squeaking wheels, the lowing of oxen and the clangorous cussing of the drovers. Above the din, Leah shouted her request to the wagonmaster.

'I don't like the idea of women travelling alone,' he'd answered her bluntly. 'Young ones anyhow. I got enough trouble with the Sioux and Cheyenne without a young gal to get the men all riled up.'

Leah blushed. 'I—I'd keep to myself.'

Alonzo Simms was the biggest man Leah had ever seen, tall and wide with a bulging girth that strained the buttons of his vest, and when he thrust his large head forward to eye her up and down, it was on a thick stump of neck. He took in the prim bonnet, the high, buttoned bodice, the corseted waist, and the long skirt, and then he scratched his head. 'Well, mebbe you ain't the kind to stir up trouble.'

'I'm meeting my grandfather at Fort Laramie,' Leah had assured him quickly. 'He's going to purchase a wagon and all the supplies we need. I was hoping I could find a place with someone else until he joins the train.'

'You can hitch up with me!'

The strident voice rang out from the far side of the shop, and Alonzo Simms and Leah turned simultaneously at the sound of it to see a short, square woman stride briskly over to them. She walked like a man and she was dressed like a man, her rough cotton trousers tucked into high boots, a bandanna around the collar of her flannel shirt. Short wisps of wiry grey hair sprang out at varying angles from under a stained felt hat.

'Birdie Gordon's the name!' She grabbed Leah's hand and pumped it vigorously. 'Used to own the best dang farm in Missouri, but I'm headin' West now—gonna sign me up on Mr Alonzo Simms' train!' And with that she thrust out one arm to give the wagonmaster a comradely whack across the middle. He bent double, letting out a furious bellow of breath, but undisturbed, Birdie Gordon went right on. 'I heard everything you and Mr Simms said, child. Now I got a wagon and four of the dumbest oxen you ever seen and high hopes— and you're welcome to share 'em all! We'll split everything fair and square, right down the middle.'

Mouth open and wide eyes fixed on the woman in wonderment, Leah hastily remembered her manners. 'Thank you, Mrs—' she paused, then quickly stuttered a correction, 'uh—Miss Gordon—'

Birdie Gordon hooted. 'Just plain Birdie! Real name's Ernestine Jean, but I plugged the last fellah who called me that.' She hooked her thumbs in her belt and rocked back on her heels. 'It's like this. I'm headin' for California to find me a husband—and I figure once you shed some of them Eastern doo-dads, you're gonna draw men like bees to honey. Well, mebbe I can lasso one of 'em as he flies by!' She clamped a hand on Leah's shoulder and looked squarely into her face. 'Well, what do you say? Is it a deal?'

Birdie Gordon was certainly nothing like the soft spoken women who gathered at the Academy for Sunday tea or Saturday afternoon concerts, but she had appeared like an angel in the midst of this noisy, dusty,

bewildering frontier town. And the blue eyes in the
blunt, seamed face were as clear and as honest as her
conversation. Leah answered without hesitation.

'I'd like very much to join you, M—Birdie!'

Birdie hooted again, louder this time, and gave Leah a
slap on the back that sent her Boston bonnet slewing
sideways. 'Glad to hear it!'

The wagonmaster ducked his head, heavy jowls
bouncing in emphasis. 'I welcome you both to the
train—but I got one question to ask.' He pushed back his
sombrero and folded the massive arms. 'Miss Cabot,
how does a city gal like you appear to be reckon she's
gonna make it on the trail? This ain't any Sunday School
picnic we're startin' on!'

It was the same question Leah had asked herself for
months—yet now she knew the answer. She drew herself
up and squared her shoulders. 'Anything I need to
know—I can learn!'

Grandfather John's words, but maybe they were hers
now, too.

'And I'm just the one to teach her,' Birdie added
firmly. 'You just wait and see, Mr Alonzo Simms—this
little gal and I are gonna make a fine team!'

And they had, those first weeks out of Missouri, as the
canvas caravan, twenty wagons strong, made its slow
way across the prairies. The rolling hills were luxuriant
with mounds of pillowy grass, thick with wildflowers,
and there was abundant wood for the cookfires and
water from clear running streams.

Those were good days, days in which to learn the
routine of the trail.

Leah Cabot learned, too, under Birdie Gordon's
tutelage. Learned to cook beans and bacon on a clumsy

tripod over an open fire. Learned to hold the reins when they forded a river, Birdie walking beside the team, oxen goad high in one hand. Learned to rise at four and to be ready to roll at seven. Learned, too, that after a whole day in the open air, she had an appetite fiercer than she'd believed possible, and that the feel of a single quilt on a hard wagon could be more welcome than a soft featherbed.

But she learned first to abandon her cumbersome Eastern garb. She purchased a wide-brimmed felt hat and a pair of sturdy boots in Independence, and made over several of her dragging dresses into divided riding skirts that fell to only boot-top length. Birdie had suggested true men's britches, but Leah had demurred at that.

'Why, back East,' she'd told the woman, 'ladies aren't even supposed to admit they have legs.'

Birdie gave a snort of derision. 'It must take 'em a powerful long time to get anyplace!'

Leah had donned her new clothes for the first time on the morning they left Independence, climbing rather self consciously up to the wagon seat. Reins in hand, Birdie had given her an enthusiastic nod of approval. 'We'll make a pioneer outta you yet, child, me and the California trail!'

Freshly painted and scrubbed, the wagons stood ready on that May morning, their canvas covers sparkling white in the sunshine, hoes and ploughs strapped to their sides, tar buckets swinging from rear axles. They stretched out a mile or more in a rocking, uneven line, small knots of loose stock—horses and oxen, milch cows and mules—clumped beside and behind the column.

Alonzo Simms had ridden his big bay gelding to the

head of that waiting line, and half standing in the stirrups, lifted one arm high in the air and pointed westward. 'Wagons, ho!'

His words were met with a whoop, 'California or bust!' The drivers lifted their reins, the oxen laid into their yokes, and the wagons rolled forward. The journey had begun—for all of them.

For the sunbonneted women in calico and the lean men in mudstained boots, their children nestled between them on the wagon seats. For the boys and girls in homespun, newly married and anxious for a new land. For the prospectors in linsey-woolsey and steeple-crowned hats. Going West, all of them—all with a shared eagerness for the Promised Land, and all with their own dreams of what that land would bring.

Except for me, Leah had thought. Except for me. I have only borrowed dreams. And can a borrowed dream sustain me the long way to California?

Yet, in the light of a new morning, it was a stranger's dreams Leah found herself thinking of.

Had some wasted dream—some cherished dream gone unfulfilled—led the man to come upon her in the stillness of the night?

The sky was barely a burgeoning pink as she climbed down from the wagon. Buried deep within the folds of the blanket she carried was the stranger's knife—she would return it to him this morning.

He was gone.

A twist of disappointment, as keen as the blade of his knife, turned within her.

He was gone, but had she really expected him to stay?

Leah turned her steps towards the edge of the encampment and beyond.

The Platte River, warm and muddy and infested with
wiggle tails, had been their only water source since
crossing into the vast plains of Nebraska. Though they'd
boiled the drinking supply, washing—for both people
and clothes—had been a sketchy affair. But yesterday
they'd made camp by an underground spring, and the
wagonmaster had granted them an extra hour this morning for a wholesale scrubbing.

Leah had discovered a small, secret bend in that
spring while filling the water bucket the night before,
and it was there she headed now. Birdie, she knew,
would be busy watering the stock and herding them
from their night corral, so she still had a few minutes
before she must begin breakfast.

Cottonwoods and willows bent low over the water,
their branches meeting overhead to form a still, se-
cluded pond. Filtered through the mesh of leaves,
the light within the small backwater was green-
gold and dim. From farther upstream the sound of
women's voices echoed softly back, but here all was
privacy.

Leah piled blanket and clothes on the bank, then
slipped off her nightshift and quickly entered the water.
Sharp needles of cold stung her skin, and she gasped for
breath, but the bite of the water held a cleansing power,
purging her of a portion of the morning's disappointment, the night's bewilderment.

She went deeper, until the water reached just above
her breasts, and dipped beneath the surface, coming
slowly up again. She smoothed back the hair from her
face, its chestnut colour spangled with auburn high-
lights, its heavy thickness lying wet and sleek against her
skin.

Through the droplets of water that clung to her lashes, she saw the stranger.

He was standing on the grassy bank, half hidden by the trees, and Leah wondered fleetingly if he was but imagined, if she'd conjured him up from her own longing.

He came forward, shirt unlaced to the waist, and as he knelt at the water's edge, she saw the quicksilver play of muscles across his chest. His beard was gone, his full, dark moustache trimmed to fit his upper lip, and she saw, too, that he was younger than she had thought at first, no more than thirty. In the dim, dappled haze, his tawny eyes—eyes she had dreamt of—were shot through with strange lights as he looked down at her, tiny lines raying out from the corners as if he'd been squinting forever into the sun.

'So you're real after all.' His eyes roamed the length of her bare throat and shoulders. 'Very real.'

A flurry of birds, wings beating hard against the branches, circled skyward, and the noise turned Leah's gaze upward, brought the man quickly to his feet again. His eyes followed the skybound birds, then dropped again to the tilted line of Leah's face.

Firm of chin and jaw, with a generous mouth and thick black brows that etched a straight line across white skin, it was a vivid face—when she let it be. And now, startled into unawareness, flushed with cold and surprise, the dark green eyes wide, the black lashes starred with water, it was an arresting face, vital and alive.

Slowly Leah returned her gaze to the man, saw his eyes narrow, saw the corded muscles of his torso go rigid with a sharp intake of breath. Saw him start into the water.

Poised for flight, she could not move. Eyes dilated with fear, she could not run. The same madness that had held her captive last night—deep within, unsuspected—held her now. Without conscious thought she lifted one hand and the motion sent the water rippling in ever widening circles around her. But whether she meant to ward him off or beckon him close, she did not know.

With the same abruptness with which he'd started towards her, the man halted.

He bent forward to splash the icy water over his face and hair, then lifted his head and shook back the moisture and, turning, moved back to the bank. He reached for the blanket and held it out behind him.

Leah hesitated a moment before clutching the blanket. Quickly she wound it tight about her.

The man stretched out full length on the slope, face to the sun. 'Name's Cole McCullough.' He folded his arms beneath his head, bent one knee. 'I discovered you by accident this morning, I was on my way to wash up.'

His husky voice was laced with a drawl, and when he continued, a joyless laugh sounded up from somewhere deep within. 'As you might have guessed, I'm in somewhat—reduced—circumstances. Or at least I was. Your wagonmaster just staked me to a horse and a gun—and gave me the job of outrider on this train.'

Leah looked at him from under lowered lashes. 'What did you tell Mr Simms about last night?'

'That I was bushwhacked and left for dead, my money and my belongings stolen. And thanks to you, he believed me.'

'Were you telling the truth?' Leah asked softly.

McCullough pushed up on an elbow, and the angular planes of his face held a feline slant. 'Maybe.'

One hand holding the coarse blanket hard to her body, Leah waded quickly from the water. She knew now that Cole McCullough was the one who'd conjured up the spell—and that she must break it. But as she stooped to retrieve her clothes, her eyes fell on his knife. Deliberately she picked it up and held it out to him, and her voice was clear and even.

'I think this is yours.'

Eyes on hers, McCullough sat up and took the knife, and when she would have straightened, he seized her wrist and pulled her close.

'Why did you help me?'

Leah knew no trick of the coquette, knew nothing of artifice or trickery. Until the previous night she'd known nothing of deception.

'I don't know,' she said simply, and in the tilt of her head, in the vivid face, there was honesty, and unconscious dignity. 'Perhaps because—in spite of everything—I trusted you.'

His eyebrows drew sharply together, as if he doubted her words, and then his reckless mouth spread wide in a grin, his teeth startlingly white beneath the dark moustache, against his swarthy skin. 'Lady, you picked the wrong man to trust!'

Leah jerked sharply away from him, his gibe like a slap in the face.

The purifying effect of the water had been but an illusion. She felt soiled—and shamed. Frenziedly Leah gathered up her clothes, her breath coming in hard, hurtful gasps. And as she ran swiftly back to camp, mocking laughter echoed behind her.

CHAPTER
TWO

FIRELIGHT cast leaping shadows on the white canvas wagon covers. The day had been long and heavy with heat. Streaks of lightning lit the horizon, the muted rumble of thunder following, but the promise of cooling rain was still far in the distance.

From nearby came the sounds of the stock in their night corral, bellows and stamps and brays, and from further on, the faint murmur of the Platte. The smell of bacon and boiled coffee lingered in the stifling air, and overall was the bittersweet wail of a fiddle.

> O Shenandoah, I long to hear you,
> Away you rolling river,
> O Shenandoah, I long to hear you,
> Away, I'm bound away,
> 'Cross the wide Missouri.

The last note hung suspended, long and lonely. Like a farewell, Leah thought. She gazed at the people gathered around the smokey campfire, their small circle centred within the larger circle of the tightly drawn up wagons. Etched on their faces, trailworn and careworn, was the pain of each private farewell.

'Play somethin' lively, Sourdough!' Birdie Gordon

leapt to her feet. 'This ain't a funeral! Play us something we can dance to!'

Sourdough O'Rourke grunted. 'Hmph. Can't stand a sassy woman.' But shifting his cigar to the other side of his mouth, he plunged into the strains of *Buffalo Gals*.

Hunkering down again on the matted patch of grass, Birdie nudged Leah and lowered her voice. 'What do you think of Sourdough? I got my sights on him as husband material.'

Leah blinked. 'Sourdough?'

The fiddler was short and wiry and swathed in an enormous apron. A battered black top hat was perched on his knobby forehead, bobbing in rhythm to his music, and the scraggle of white whiskers lining his cheeks was broken in two by the black cigar.

'I know he ain't much to look at.' Birdie sighed. 'And he's ornery as a mule. But he does the cookin' for the wagonmaster's mess—and I like the idea of a husband who can cook!'

Leah laughed aloud. It felt wonderful to laugh, to savour these moments of ease. There were few such moments on the trail these days.

Excepting the scanty patches of willows and cotton-woods that grew on the silty islands in the Platte, or on the banks of the infrequent streams, the thin soil of Nebraska was barren of trees. And without trees, there was no shade, no relief from the muggy heat of the plains. Without trees there was no shelter from the wind, the relentless, constant wind of the plains that reddened your eyes and choked your throat.

And without trees there was no wood—and that meant another lesson for Leah to learn. She must learn to hide her nausea as she gathered the chips of buffalo dung that, when dried, were their only source of fuel.

But now was not the time to think of the dust and the heat and the hard jostling of the wagon seat—now was the time to forget the day just spent and all the days that lay waiting.

Women sat gossiping, idly swatting at bugs while their menfolk traded tales of the land ahead and their children dashed here and there, dogs at their heels. Several couples were dancing, a kind of dance Leah had never seen before. They'd formed squares on the dusty buffalo grass and were whirling and curtseying and promenading to Sourdough's shouted orders.

'Bow to your corner and do-si-do, then you allemande left, don't ya know!'

Leah drew back into the shadows, arms clasped around her drawn up knees. This was her first campfire. She'd kept apart from the others on the train—she held no share in their common dream, she had no right to share in their companionship. But tonight at dinner Birdie had urged her to join in.

'It'll do you good,' she'd asserted flatly, tin plate in one hand, tin cup in the other. 'Lord knows you deserve a bit of fun—Lord knows we all do!'

And so Leah had come. Partly to satisfy Birdie, partly because the long night after the long day stretched out drearily.

Mainly because she knew there was a chance that Cole McCullough might be there too.

He was gone from camp most days, riding out early with Jeremy Fisher, pilot on the train, to scout the trail ahead, locate likely campsites, hunt fresh meat. He returned late or not at all, spending sometimes several days on a forage.

Mounted, his was an immediately recognisable figure—completely different from the rangy sodbusters who jostled awkwardly on their horses. As if he'd been wedded to it at an early age, he lounged gracefully in the saddle, stetson slouched low over one eye, big shoulders moving against his buckskin.

In camp his was an unmistakable figure as well. Unmistakable, powerful—solitary.

Whether leaving or returning from a scout, he always reined in well behind Jeremy Fisher, whether riding the line or tending to the horses, he moved alone. Leah knew well how alone, for she found herself watching him—as he bent to his chores, as he rode out in the mornings—watching him until he was a distant shadow on the horizon.

He never noticed her. Never sought her out. Never spoke to her. Never gave any indication that he remembered their first meeting and the morning after. And perhaps, she'd told herself over and over, he didn't. Perhaps he'd known a hundred such moments and mornings. Whereas she had been allowed only those few.

It was all so bewildering. Why should her eyes follow him? Why should she feel that keen edge of disappointment when he ignored her? Why should her heart hammer when she remembered the look in his eyes as she'd knelt by his side in the night?

Always before her emotions had been dictated to her—like her chores for the day—loyalty to the school, devotion to duty. But those second-hand emotions were as nothing compared to the feelings Cole McCullough evoked in her.

Always before her male companionship had been

limited to those few men Grandfather John had deemed suitable, handed down to her like the marketing list. They'd accompanied her to church, escorted her to museums, but she'd never watched for their coming, waited for their words.

Yes, it was very bewildering. Why should her heart stir and lift as it had today, when she'd seen Cole McCullough ride early into the camp, pack horse behind him laden with fresh meat, buffalo and antelope? Why should there be the curious flutter in her stomach at the sight of him now, leaning against one of the wagons, one booted leg crossed carelessly over the other?

His head was bent low, and as Leah watched, he wiped his pistol with his bandanna, then checked the spare cylinders. Abruptly he pushed back the brim of his stetson with the tip of his revolver. His head lifted, his gaze surprising Leah's own, and cheeks flaming scarlet, she looked quickly away.

Sourdough finished the reel with a flourish and sent a snort of satisfaction in Birdie's direction. 'Was that lively enough fer ya, Miz Gordon?'

Faces flushed from heat and exertion, the dancers clapped and stomped for another song, and Sourdough scowled at them.

'All right, all right! Jest give me a dang minute!' He rolled the cigar to the other side of his mouth, wiped his hands on the dirty apron, and then held fiddle and bow aloft. 'What'll it be?'

'How about *Dixie*?'

Silence met McCullough's words, self-conscious silence with a hushed undercurrent running beneath it. The dancers shuffled their feet and exchanged glances, and those seated put their heads together and whispered behind lifted hands.

Cole McCullough came slowly into the circle and the smokey light of the campfire threw his shadow against the wagon covers. 'I said—how about *Dixie*?'

Dixie. A tumult of memories ran through Leah's brain. Micah in his uniform, Grandfather John's face as he read and re-read the casualty list—

One of the children, standing wide eyed and unsure at the grown-ups' silence, blurted out, 'But that's a Reb song!'

'Hush!' His mother drew the child quickly aside.

'The young'un's right, McCullough.' Sourdough bit down decisively on his cigar. 'I ain't played *Dixie* since the war started.'

'Well, the war's over!' Birdie called out firmly. She stood and strode up to the fiddler, giving him a whack across the shoulders so hardy it sent him stumbling forward, cigar spilling from his mouth, bow falling from his fingers. 'And there ain't no finer tune for dancin'!'

Sourdough went nose to nose with the woman. 'I swore I'd never fiddle that song again!'

Birdie stooped and picked up cigar and bow. With a firm hand she stuffed the cigar in the fiddler's mouth. With an equally firm hand she jabbed the bow in his middle. 'Play!'

Sourdough was obviously a man who knew when he was licked. Muttering cusses—but softly—he took up the bow and crashed into *Dixie*.

Dixie. Leah's hands tightened. The last time she'd heard the song had been the night of the surrender. They'd played it in the streets, mockingly, derisively, as the victory bonfires crackled. But for some, the victory had come too late—

'Dance, Miss Cabot?'

McCullough gave her no time for protest, taking her hands in his and pulling her to her feet.

She arched her body away from him. 'I mustn't dance to this!'

'Mustn't? That's a strange choice of words. Does that mean perhaps you want to, but think you shouldn't?'

'It means—' She stopped blankly. Her thoughts were suddenly whirling as fast as the music, blurring the images in her brain. What did it mean? She was no longer sure.

She only knew that Grandfather John would disapprove—but he was miles and days down the trail.

Cole laughed and swung her into the circle of his arms, and the protesting arc of her body bent easily before his strength. Quickly she averted her gaze.

'I—I've never danced a reel before—'

'You'll do fine. Follow me.'

They were the only couple moving to the music, and she was conscious of the watching eyes, conscious that always before her dancing had been limited to staid waltzes with stiff partners.

Conscious, too, of the scent that clung to his clothes, hickory smoke and leather, as different from the bookish, stale odour of the men she'd always known as the brown, sunburnt colour of his skin was from their pale mustiness, as different as his buckskin was from their broadcloth. He lifted her high, twirling her around, and she felt the play of his muscles beneath that buckskin.

'What happened to the girl at the spring?'

'I—I don't understand—'

'You look enough like that girl to be her twin, but you aren't her. She was alive—the girl I've seen these weeks on the trail is as stiff as a spinster on a Sunday morning.'

Leah made a quick sound of protest. Hurt and angry, she tried to jerk away from him, but he held her firm. And once again came that abrupt command.

'Look at me.'

And once again, driven by the force of his voice, Leah obeyed. The firelight was leaping across his dark face, and moving in the amber depths of his eyes was a strange challenge.

'The girl I saw that first night—and at the spring—she was soft and her eyes were tender. Her hair fell loose. But you wear your hair all scalped off your face—you hold your body tight and stiff. What are you frightened of?'

She was breathless, not from the dance, but from his words. 'I don't know what you mean—'

'I think you do know,' Cole said softly. He pulled her closer yet. 'Tell me—what are you frightened of?'

The question pounded at her, but she had no answer. Or was there an answer, dimly felt, as through the darkness of a night sky studded with stars? Dimly seen, as through a haze of morning sunlight, filtered gold and green? Was there an answer, but buried so deep she was afraid to find it?

The retort of a Winchester fired skyward halted the music, shattered the moment, broke it into fragments, and spilled them on the ground. Leah stumbled mid-step, the sound seeming to explode in her ears. Still in Cole McCullough's arms, she saw over his shoulder a tall, gangly-limbed man with a rifle in his hands and hatred on his face.

'I heard me enough of that Reb music!'

'Keep playing, Sourdough,' McCullough said steadily, 'the lady and I haven't finished dancing.'

Bow poised over his fiddle, cigar working rapidly in his mouth, Sourdough shifted his gaze between the two men. Those about the campfire looked from one to the other as well, and the silence now was stark, as heavy as the heat.

'Eb Hutter! Didn't you hear what I said?' Birdie elbowed her way into the centre of the circle. 'The war's over!'

Hands on hips, the woman cast a glance around the fire. 'We're headin' fer the Promised Land, right? Fer a new future? Well, then, ain't it time we fergit the past?'

'Some of us'll never fergit!'

Hutter slammed the stock of his rifle hard against the ground, the hooded eyes in the flat, beaked face narrowing. 'I lost two boys at Shiloh and four years of my life to the war—I'd as soon kill a Johnny Reb as look at one.' He shot out a yellowed stream of tobacco juice, then wiped his mouth on the back of his hand and took a step towards McCullough. 'And I say anyone who wants to hear *Dixie* is a Johnny Reb.'

Cole didn't turn, but his hands fell from Leah's waist, and she saw the heavy line of his shoulders tense.

'Eb—' A thin, whey-faced woman put one hand on Hutter's sleeve. 'Don't make no trouble—'

'Git away, Abigail!' Impatiently Hutter shrugged his wife aside. 'I'm askin' you plain, McCullough. When we licked the Rebs, were you wearin' blue—or grey?'

'I was wearing buckskin,' Cole answered levelly, 'and killing Apaches.' He paused, and like a cat readying itself to pounce, held the strength of his body coiled taut

a moment before swinging slowly around. 'And anything else about me, Mr Hutter—' the husky voice
softened, and sharpened, 'is none of your damn business.'

From beyond the wagons came a hoarse shout and the
night guard burst pell mell into the circle. Red faced,
eyes bulging, he extended one arm behind him. 'Injuns!'

And even as he spoke the word, a line of coppery-
skinned, straight-backed men, no more than six or
seven, rode slowly into the camp.

Their nakedness was startling. Except for one who
wore a buffalo robe draped over his shoulder, they were
clad only in breechclouts, pieces of fur and tanned skin
plaited in black hair that bristled with feathers. They
straddled their mounts bareback, the sound of their
horses' hooves effectively muffled with rawhide wrap-
pings.

'Well, glory be.' For once Birdie's voice was subdued.
'Looks like we got company.'

McCullough pushed forward. His hand went quickly
to his holster—though he did not draw—and a shiver of
apprehension rippled up Leah's spine. These were the
first Indians they had encountered, but they'd all heard
the stories of savage massacres, fiendish tortures. The
eye of every man, woman, and child was held by the still,
mounted file.

Yet save for the knives they wore at their belts, these
men were unarmed and wore no war paint. And far
from being screaming madmen, they were sombre eyed,
their silence as great as that of the people they faced, and
their broad faces impassive.

The guard's shout had brought Alonzo Simms at a run
from his wagon, and obviously from a sound sleep as

well. He wore no boots, though he'd managed to jam on the giant sombrero, and his suspenders flopped loose over red flannel underwear.

'Pawnee,' the wagonmaster muttered to McCullough from one side of his mouth, hitching up his trousers as he spoke. 'Touchiest tribe on the plains. I had a hunch they were around, that's why I sent Fisher out tonight to cut their sign. Instead they came callin' on us!' He jabbed furiously at his hat. 'We're in a devil of a fix. Pawnees got too much pride to learn our tongue and I don't know their lingo.'

McCullough took a few measured strides forward, eyes never leaving the silent line of Indians. 'Tell me what you want to say—I speak their sign language.'

'Well, I'll be—' Alonzo Simms pushed back the brim of his sombrero and gave the heavy head a shake. 'You might just make me glad I hired you, McCullough!'

Shifting from one foot to the other, the wagonmaster began. 'Tell 'em I'm the head of this outfit—the chief—'

As the big man spoke, Cole matched his words with a series of deliberate hand movements.

'Tell 'em we mean 'em no harm,' Simms continued, 'tell 'em that we respect the Pawnee, that we want their friendship.'

When McCullough finished, the brave in the buffalo robe began his own signing.

'His name is Two Hatchet,' Cole translated, 'and he's the chief of this band of Pawnee.' His voice was loud enough for all to hear, and at the even sound of it, Leah allowed some of the tension to drain from her. She looked at the Indian with less suspicion and more curiosity, and saw that where McCullough's every gesture had been firm and definite, Two Hatchet's motions were fluent, the gracefulness of his hands strangely at odds with his stoic demeanour.

'He says that this is their land and their buffalo,' McCullough went on. 'And they demand a tribute from us for crossing their land and killing their buffalo.'

'The hell they do!'

With the hard jab of an elbow, Eb Hutter shoved Cole aside and levelled his Winchester at the mounted braves. 'A belly full of lead is all you'll get from us, you heathen savages!'

'You fool!' Spinning swiftly, Cole crashed his fist into Hutter's face to send him sprawling backwards, the rifle falling from his hands and plummeting to the ground beside him. 'They came in peace!'

There was fury in the stiffening of the near-naked bodies, fury in the sudden rigid widening of Two Hatchet's eyes and in the quivering of his flared nostrils. He jerked the knife from his belt and hurtled it at one of the wagons. And as the blade slashed through the canvas cover, Leah felt the skin at the back of her scalp tighten convulsively.

Sourdough let out a low whistle. 'No need to translate that.'

'Tell 'em we're mighty sorry,' Simms whispered urgently. 'Tell 'em we'll give 'em all the tribute he wants—a pound of sugar and flour for each of his braves!'

Hutter made a surly sound of protest and started forward, but Sourdough grabbed his shirt and yanked him back. 'Shut up,' the fiddler growled, 'you've made enough trouble.'

Two Hatchet returned the wagonmaster's words with

abbreviated gestures, as hard as the set of his body, and
Cole shook his head.

'Supplies aren't going to do it. We've insulted his
pride—and he wants a tribute equal to that insult.'

'How about some kind of flashy trinket?' The wagonmaster wiped his streaming forehead on the sleeve of his
union suit. 'Jewellery maybe?'

McCullough passed one hand under his chin consideringly. 'Maybe. What's important is that Two Hatchet
feel the gift is a sacrifice—that the white man who gives it
is giving something of himself. That's the only way he
can save his pride.'

'And we can save our skins,' Sourdough muttered. He
nodded to the Indian. 'We'd better git on with pow wow.
Looks like Two Hatchet's about to pull out—and the
next time he and his braves come callin', you can be dang
certain they'll be wearin' war paint.'

'I may have something—'

The sound of her voice surprised Leah, but she didn't
hesitate. Quickly she slid a gold chain up from under her
bodice and unfastened the clasp. The small medallion
she held out for McCullough's inspection gleamed gold
and bore an inscription.

'It was given to my great-great-grandfather by the
mayor of Boston,' Leah said swiftly, 'in appreciation for
the founding of Cabot Academy.'

Cole looked briefly at the medal, then raised his eyes to
her face and his glance narrowed. He turned and began
again to sign to the Indian, translating as his hands
framed the words.

'I'm telling them the medal belonged to an elder of
your family. That it was given to him by a respected chief
of your tribe. That it means much to you—but that you

offer it as a token of respect for the Pawnee and their chief.'

The Indian answered, nodded once, and extended a brown, bare arm to Leah.

'He wants you to give the gift to him,' McCullough said quietly, 'that way the sacrifice will be complete.' And as if to confirm his own words, Two Hatchet dismounted and stood waiting.

Leah's stomach knotted, her brief flame of courage turning to the ashes of fear, she swung distraught eyes to Cole McCullough. But there was no way to tell him, no way to make him understand that she'd been raised to go quietly about her days, trained to move in the shadows, to serve, not to step boldly forward, not to meet life head on.

'I can't—'

He stepped close, his words for her hearing alone. 'The girl I knew on that first night had the courage to do anything.'

And as on that first night, she felt the warmth of his gaze. He did not speak it, but she heard his words of assurance. They did not touch, but she sensed the ready support in that powerful body.

Leah lifted her head and started forward.

A sudden gust of wind held the scent of rain, a sudden flash of lightning directly overhead illumined the night sky and the scene below. The silent, staring file of Indians, their chief standing as a statue cast in bronze. The watching circle gathered tight around the campfire, the man in buckskin at their head. The girl walking slowly forward, her grace of movement singular and unconscious.

Leah halted before the Indian. A pungent smell—

faintly like bacon grease, but sharper—met her nostrils. She looked clearly into the strongly marked face, saw the coppery skin stretched tight over the high cheek-bones. She looked full into his eyes, black and deep and fathomless. There was a dignity about this man that, somehow, reminded her of Grandfather John.

John Cabot. The medal had been one of his most valued possessions, entrusted reluctantly to her before he started West.

But she must not think of that now. She arched the slender neck and threw back her head, feeling the heavy weight of her hair in its tight knot. She extended her hand, and the medal resting in her palm was warm from the touch of her skin.

Two Hatchet reached out a single forefinger to trace it slowly down the curve of her cheek. She did not flinch from his touch, but stood steadily, and the Indian raised his head, speaking again through the strangely fluent, oddly elegant motions of his hands.

But this time McCullough did not translate, and bewildered, Leah half turned to see Cole point decisively to himself. Whatever had passed between them, Two Hatchet seemed satisfied. He took the medallion from Leah, holding it high over his head to show his braves. At their nods of approval he hung it around his neck and swung up onto his horse, signing a last few words.

McCullough lifted his voice. 'He says we're free to travel his land! And he thanks us for the gift.'

Two Hatchet raised one flat-palmed hand level with his chest and McCullough returned the salute. Without a backward glance, and as silently as they had come, the line of Pawnee rode into the night.

The shrill buzz of conversation washed over the camp,

the people breaking from their circle like insects from the hive, knotting into small groups to recount what had just happened.

'My thanks to you, Miz Cabot,' Mrs Hutter nodded diffidently, and beyond her Leah saw others of the train, awkwardly touching the brims of their stained hats, smiling shyly and nodding. And Birdie was there, too, to give her a wink.

'You did real fine, child.'

'She sure did.' The wagonmaster took off the sombrero to wipe his face again, clamped it back on and blew out his cheeks. 'Little lady, you just saved us a tangle of trouble!'

Another burst of lightning lit the sky, and against the following thunder, Simms bellowed, 'Back to your wagons! We're in for a heavy night of it!'

A gust of wind swirled the dust high and thick in the air, overturned a water barrel and rocked the wagons, and the people scattered as if blown before the wind themselves, Indians forgotten in the newer need of meeting the storm.

Sourdough slammed one hand atop his battered black hat, holding it firm. 'If it ain't one blamed thing it's another.'

'Quit your grousin',' Birdie nudged the fiddler cheerfully in the ribs. 'We still got our scalps, ain't we?'

The wagonmaster threw back his head, as big and shaggy as a buffalo's, and roared in laughter. 'Birdie Gordon, you are the doggonedest woman!'

'Can't stand a sassy woman,' Sourdough grumbled, stomping along in the wagonmaster's wake.

A volley of thunder shook the air, and head down against the wind, Birdie started away. 'Come on, child!'

She gestured back to Leah. 'That rain ain't gonna hold off forever!'

Leah nodded absently, but didn't follow. She wanted a few moments alone to sort out these new feelings.

On her own—unbidden, unasked—she'd attempted something fine and strong and she'd succeeded! The sweetness of victory, unfelt until that night, was sweeping her senses like the hard rush of the wind. And mingled with the tang of victory, was the niggling thought—small, but persistent—that perhaps there was a place for her on this trek westward.

The rain was beginning and she tilted back her head to feel the fullness of the drops on her face. They were cool and light. Reluctantly she started for the wagon and, as she turned, a spike of lightning rent the sky. Against the sudden, brief brilliance the figure of Cole McCullough stood clearly outlined—and this time, he was watching her.

The rain that began with a murmur against the wagon covers turned into a deluge by morning. Nor did it end that day, but continued on through the next, and the day after that. Sullen rain, that soaked through canvas and blankets and clothes. Dreary rain, that deadened the spirits.

The wagons rolled steadily—if slowly—on. The rain did settle the dust, only to raise the mosquitoes, and it did leave the grass thick and green for grazing. But it also left the mud. By the fourth morning—the first to dawn clear in as many days—the trail was all but impassable.

'Come on! Buck, Blue! Come on, you mangy, worthless, no-good, flea-bit, pea-brained critters, come on!'

Kneeling in the wagon bed to pack away the remains

of breakfast, Leah heard Birdie bawl out the string of commands to the oxen. Similar shouts rang out up and down the line, as men and women struggled to dislodge their rigs from the mud. Leah stowed away the grub box and crawled out to the seat. The wagon bows were hooped to a height of barely five feet and inside, only the children could stand erect.

'Confound it!' Birdie kicked at a wheel. She stood ankle deep in mud, an oxen goad in one hand and an angry scowl on the seamed face. 'I can't move these blamed critters an inch!'

Leah hiked up her split skirt and slid to the ground. 'Let me help.'

'I don't know—' Birdie ran her eyes over Leah's figure, neatly rounded but slim. 'You're a mite scrawny.'

In unintentional imitation of one of Birdie's favourite gestures, Leah put her hands firmly on her hips. 'You said back in Independence we were going to split things fair and square. Well, doesn't that mean the mud, too?'

Birdie slapped the felt hat down flat against her head in sudden decision. 'I guess it does!' She cupped her palms, spit once in each and rubbed them on the back of her britches. 'You push and I'll pull and we'll get you to Fort Laramie yet!'

Leah grinned. There was something cheering about Birdie. Something that made her feel able to take on the mud—and the world!

All at once, Leah wondered what Grandfather John would think of Birdie Gordon.

She lifted her chin. It didn't matter what he thought. This was one time he would have to defer to her judgment. She was keeping Birdie as a friend. And as Leah sloshed through the mired ruts to take her place at a rear wheel, she was amazed at the temerity of her own thoughts.

'Git! Buck, Blue, git I say! Duke! Mose! Git!'

Birdie tugged on the lines, prodding the team with the goad, and the oxen bellowed and skittered. As Leah shoved against the wheel, she heard the dull, slogging sound of horse's hooves and looked up to see Cole McCullough grinning down at her. He was stripped to the waist, bandanna around his neck, and his buckskin breeches and the broad expanse of chest were spattered with mud.

'Having some trouble, Miss Cabot?'

Leah doubled her efforts, gasping out her answer through gritted teeth. 'We'll manage.'

McCullough dismounted swiftly. He strode to the rear of the wagon, leaning one shoulder against it, and with this new strength to aid them, the oxen strained forward. Slowly, slowly, inch by sloughing inch, the wheels slid up and out of the mud.

Leah straightened wearily, passing a hand across her forehead. Half-turning, her eyes fell on Cole. He stood head down, arms extended, hands flat against the wagon. The line of his face showed gaunt hollows, giving the lean profile a hungry, predatory look. The line of his body showed the heavy shoulders heaving slightly, showed the sinew and thew of chest and arms, brown and rock hard and glistening with sweat.

Unaccountably she remembered his words. 'What are you frightened of?'

For a space of only a heartbeat or two, her glance held, those heartbeats thudding against her rib cage with queer excitement—yet in those brief moments, she knew she'd come perilously close to the answer. Knew that it was the very answer itself that frightened her—

She swung swiftly around, meeting Birdie head-on as the woman rounded the wagon triumphantly.

'Jehosaphat!' She hooted in jubilation. 'We did it, child!'

Leah shook her head and took a step aside. 'We have Mr McCullough to thank, Birdie.'

At the sight of Cole, Birdie gave a snort of rueful laughter. 'I'll be dadgummed.' She whacked a fist against one thigh. 'Well, whoever done it, I reckon we all oughtta celebrate! And I got just the thing.'

Birdie hoisted herself up into the wagon and a moment later an earthenware jug was extended through the canvas cover. 'This here's the best sippin' whiskey in Missouri—and I should know. I brewed it myself!' She leapt to the ground and handed the jug to Cole, and there was pride in her voice. 'It's got a kick like a mule.'

McCullough arched one eyebrow, a corner of his mouth lifting in tandem. Wordlessly, deliberately, he held the jug out to Leah.

There was wry mockery in the ridged slant of his face and a question—and again the words drummed in her brain. 'What are you frightened of?'

Leah seized the vessel in both hands and lifted it to her lips to drink long and deeply. Tears sprung to her eyes as the whiskey scalded her mouth, and the fire burned all the way to the pit of her stomach.

Birdie took back the jug and squinted at Leah curiously. 'Ever had a drink of hooch before?'

Leah shook her head, afraid she'd shoot flames if she answered, and Birdie thumped her on the back. 'Well, you took your medicine good and proper! First swallow's always the hardest.' The woman took a hearty swig of the whiskey herself, smacking her lips in appreciation, then passed the jug once more to Cole. He tilted back his head to take a hard drink, and Birdie nodded at him.

'Thanks for your help today, Mr McCullough. I reckon that's how the good Lord means us to get to California—each one helping the other.'

'I helped you because it was my job,' Cole said levelly. He handed her the jug. 'I don't happen to care very much if this train gets to California or if it doesn't.'

'Mebbe you don't,' Birdie answered him bluntly. 'But everyone needs help.' She paused, and the blue eyes in the square face appraised him steadily. 'Even you.'

A finger crooked through the handle, Birdie balanced the jug over one shoulder and started around again towards the front of the wagon. 'Get set for a snort of my best brew, you darlin' animals! That oughtta get you to the Promised Land in one piece!'

Back propped against a wagon bow, Leah watched Birdie's retreating figure under half lowered lids. The feverish heat had subsided to a wonderful warmth, and it was winding languorously through her body. She shifted her gaze to Cole. He was grinning at her again, and she gave him a lazy smile.

She'd heard his words. He'd said he didn't care. But then she'd already known that—known since the beginning.

She should go—she should follow Birdie—but she didn't want to move. The warmth was easing the ache in her shoulders, the stiffness in her neck. Yet it was also, curiously enough, making her strangely lightheaded. She had the uneasy feeling that Grandfather John would not want her drowsing like this in the company of a man.

Especially a man like Cole McCullough. A man who didn't care—about anything.

Resolutely, Leah stood, noting with some surprise that her legs were wobbly, took a step, slipped—and fell headlong into the mud.

'Miss Cabot,' McCullough squatted beside her, whispering conspiratorially in her ear, 'I think you're slightly tipsy.'

Leah pushed up to her knees, furiously spitting out the gritty taste of the mud. 'I am n—' but a hiccup punctuated her words.

Chuckling, Cole stood again and took her hands, but she pulled back from him, losing her balance in the process. His arms went around her waist and he lifted her to her feet. She swayed against him, and beneath her hands, his chest was firm and sure—

Leah stumbled back a step and began rubbing fiercely at the mud on her skirt.

'If you wait awhile,' Cole offered dryly, 'it'll brush off.'

Leah lifted her head. 'Thank you,' she answered with formality. She took a breath and shook back her hair, congratulating herself on how well she was recovering her dignity, when a mosquito landed on her cheek. She slapped angrily at it. Mosquitoes and mud and Cole McCullough's insolence! The exasperations of the morning piled one on top of the other and she clenched her fists at her sides and shrieked. 'Oh!'

Cole laughed aloud and, seething, Leah bent and scooped up a handful of mud and threw it squarely at him. He ducked easily.

'What a rare display—the prim Miss Cabot with her temper up.'

'I do not have a temper!' Leah shouted.

Or at least she'd never had one before. What was happening to her? She'd drunk spirits and acted like a wanton and lost a temper she'd never even known she had.

Her head was throbbing now, and she leaned back against the wagon bow and shut her eyes. She hiccuped again—and her humiliation was complete.

Pulling off his bandanna, McCullough leaned forward to wipe at the streaks of mud on her face, and there was an edge of amusement in his voice. 'I wonder what your suitor would think of you now.'

'My wh-what?'

'Two Hatchet.' He turned her head to wipe at one cheek. 'He wanted to buy you.'

Leah's eyes snapped open and her mouth dropped. Lips twisting into a dry grin, Cole set one finger under her chin and closed it firmly. 'The old devil offered two horses and a buffalo robe for you.' He pushed the bandanna into her hand. 'Finish the job, you wouldn't want people to see a proper Boston lady covered with mud.' Turning, he started for his horse.

For a moment, Leah stood stock still, bandanna in her open hand. And then she shook off her astonishment.

'Mr McCullough!' Determinedly, if a bit unsteadily, Leah ploughed towards him. Whether it was the whiskey or weariness, the mud seemed to drag at her like quicksand.

Cole swung up into the saddle, took the slouch hat from the pommel and settled it on his head. The slanted brim hid his eyes as he looked down at Leah.

'Two Hatchet,' she panted, 'what did you say to him? I—I mean when he—'

'I didn't want to offend his pride,' McCullough answered her carelessly, 'so I told him you weren't for sale.' He touched a heel to his horse, turning him. 'I said you were my woman.'

CHAPTER
THREE

THE wagons rolled on, up the sandy banks of the North Platte. The prairie spread wide before them, but now and then the land gave a foretaste of the mountains ahead.

Jutting sandstone bluffs began to crop up beside the trail, landmarks of earth and rock already christened by earlier travellers. Courthouse Rock, a many-layered mound of clay and volcanic ash that thrust up 400 feet against the sky. Chimney Rock, its stone shaft spiralling upwards like a church steeple.

But these natural wonders paled in significance before the man-made structure that lay two months down the trail.

The adobe walls first appeared on the western horizon as a dim shadow set within the angle of two rivers. But as the wagons lumbered ever closer, the shadow had stretched outward and upward to become a guiding beacon.

Fort Laramie.

Fort Laramie, the final touchstone of civilization on the way West, its picketed walls offering a day of rest and—most importantly—fresh supplies from the sutler's store.

The caravan had lost sight of it for most of that day, caught since early morning within the reaches of a steepsided bluff. But near sundown they had finally rounded past the sandstone walls to see again the eagerly awaited oasis rising above rolling river hills.

Only this time the sight was a chilling one.

The blockhouse that guarded the gate was bereft of sentries. The sky that topped the turreted ramparts was red with flame. And swirling around and about the hollow rectangle of the stockade was a funnel of smoke that darkened with every passing minute.

Leah sat tautly forward on the wagon seat, squinting hard against the setting sun, straining to see—to know— to understand.

'Birdie—' Was that dry croak her voice? Leah licked her lips but they remained cotton dry. 'Birdie, what do you think has happened?'

'Don't rightly know.' Birdie gave the lines a hard jerk, trying to hold the skittish oxen still. 'But waitin' to find out is drivin' these good for nothin' critters plumb loco—and me, too!'

Waiting . . . Leah twisted her hands in her lap with the agony of it. For somewhere within that adobe inferno was Grandfather John.

And Cole McCullough.

Having first bidden the wagons draw up at the foot of the hill that led to the Fort, Alonzo Simms had then ridden up that small sweep of land himself. And behind him, lounging carelessly in the saddle of his black, clean-limbed gelding, right hand resting easily on the butt of his holstered revolver, had ridden Cole.

Leah had almost hated him at that moment. Hated him for his detachment. Hated him all the more for she knew that her hatred of him was bound up with her fear for him. Knew, too, that had he known of her fear-riddled hatred, he would have laughed at it—and at her.

The wagonmaster's great dun broke from the Fort, the hard, rhythmic sound of horse's hooves pounding across Leah's thoughts. The thunder of those hoofbeats and the thudding of her heart became one, and she knew that these last minutes of waiting were the worst agony of all.

Simms took the slope at a dead run, horse and rider bobbing brown against the blood-red rays of the dying sun. He galloped his mount down the line of wagons, punching out his words in short, swift volleys.

'Indians and white renegades—raided the Fort! Torched it! The sutler's store is goin' up!' He wheeled the dun sharply around, turning back in the saddle to wave the wagons on even as he urged his horse forward with a touch of spurs to its flanks. 'We need every hand—we've got to save them supplies!'

In tandem the entire line of white canvas moved in response to Simms' frantic orders. The wagons jounced over the rough road, clouds of brown dust billowing out behind as the teams gathered speed.

'Haw! Haw!'

Feet braced wide and bellowing like a bullwhacker, Birdie leaned into the lines. She slapped the reins fiercely over the oxen's backs, goading them to a faster gait. The wagon lurched from side to side, creaking and shaking. Leah gripped the bow above with one hand, the jockey box with the other, her teeth rattling with every bone-jarring jerk of the iron-rimmed wheels. The felt hat slipped from her head to bounce against her back, its rawhide thongs tightening about her neck. The heavy chestnut hair fell from its pins to tumble to her waist.

The wagons rocked through the gate and into the stockade. Spread before them was a crazy quilt of soldiers in heat-scorched uniforms, trappers and traders in sweat-blackened buckskin, all passing buckets frantically from hand to hand. Their tangle of crisscrossed lines radiated outward from the north corner of the quadrangle where a small row of wooden shanties formed a tunnel of flame. The men were shouting orders to one another and to the newly arriving settlers, the rising and falling torrent of their voices punctuated by the crackling of timbers falling to the blaze.

Birdie hauled back on the reins, jerking the oxen to a halt, and Leah hastened to climb down. It was then she saw the body.

The soldier lay face down . . . a shorn and bloody cavity where the top of his head should have been. And beside him—another body—and another—

Eyes rounding in disbelief, Leah looked down the length of the stockade to see a line of still figures stretching across the hard packed earth. She went white to the lips, unable to stifle a hard gasp of revulsion.

Swiftly Birdie turned to take Leah's hand within her own blunt-fingered grasp. There was comfort there and Leah clung to it, her nails digging white half-moons into Birdie's calloused palms.

'Those poor men,' Leah murmured in mingled pity and horror, eyes lingering on the still shapes sprawled out grotesquely in the dust. 'To die like that—'

'Pull yourself together, child,' Birdie ordered brusquely. 'It's a tolerable shame 'bout those men, but there's nothin' we can do to help them poor devils—and there's a powerful lot we can do to help ourselves!

Namely savin' them supplies that's goin' get us to California!'

Leah winced at the bluntness of Birdie's words, but they carried the ring of unmistakable truth. There was a task to be done, but it was something she alone must do. She looked up from the death-strewn field, saying faintly but firmly, 'I've got to find my Grandfather. I've got to know if he's—all right.'

Birdie bobbed her head once in vigorous approval. 'I had a notion you'd say somethin' like that—reckon I'd feel the same if it was my Grandpa! But you'd best take this—' She pulled a long-barrelled pistol from her belt and thrust it into Leah's hand. 'Just in case any of them renegades is still somewheres around.'

Leah ran her fingers over the weapon with a shivering respect. 'I—I don't know if I could use it—'

'Don't stop to think about it and you'll do fine!'

Birdie leapt to the ground. She swung around, fetching down the water bucket from the tailgate, then called up a last command. 'And don't worry 'bout aimin'. If you're close enough, you're sure to hit somethin'!'

Moving at a brisk lope, Birdie's squared-off figure blended in and disappeared within the ranks of the bucket brigade—and Leah realised she was alone.

How was she to find Grandfather John in this tumult of heat and noise and flame?

Was he obscured somewhere within the smokey haze that rose up from the far corner of the stockade? Was he standing shoulder to shoulder with the others in one of those scattered, frantic lines that spliced the quadrangle? Or was he—was he lying face down in the dust, a red stain seeping across his raw scalp?

Get on with it! Leah ordered herself through set teeth.

This was not the time to sit wringing her hands, worrying over idle fancies like the proper Miss Cabot of Boston!

Why, Cole McCullough had taunted her with just those words. She heard again the mockery in the drawling voice, saw again the challenge in the dark, lean face. And the memory was like a tonic, flooding her with renewed purpose.

With sudden decision, Leah yanked off the felt hat and sent it flying into the wagon bed. She climbed to the ground, turning to see a hurrying figure in a blue uniform. Quickly she called out to him.

'Please, stop! Please—sir!'

The soldier pivoted impatiently at her words, forearming the sweat from his face. 'Ma'am?'

'I'm looking for John Cabot. Do you know him, know where I might find him?'

'Cabot's been bunkin' at the officers' quarters, ma'am.' The soldier thrust out his arm in the direction of a two-storey frame building. 'Yonder. Heard tell he was there when the renegades hit. Took a real bad shot.'

'Thank you,' Leah said automatically.

The young soldier sped off, leaving Leah staring after his retreating figure, his words reverberating in her brain. Took a real bad shot—

Leah rallied grimly. All the more reason to hurry.

The several yards between wagon and barracks were littered with bodies and spattered with blood, and the stench of death rose up to mingle with the acrid smell of smoke. Deliberately Leah focused her gaze on the shattered second-floor windows. She tightened her gingerish grip on the pistol and began rapidly forward.

Not until she stepped onto the wooden planking of the verandah did Leah realise she'd been holding her breath. She shut her eyes momentarily, letting the air escape from her lungs with a whoosh. With the toe of one boot she nudged open the door.

Here was another world, cool and dim and strangely distant from the flaming world outside. Here the silence was penetrated only by the slow creaking of the door as it swung back and forth on rusty hinges, the clamour of men's voices urgent no longer, but muffled and vague.

'Grandfather!'

Leah's plea fell hollowly, dying away without an answer. She darted an anxious glance about the room. Upturned cots and tables lined the windows, the makeshift barricades looming up in the unlit half darkness of twilight like crouching animals.

'Grandfather John!'

Still there was no response.

Across the room a flight of stairs faded into the murky depths above, and Leah started towards it. The door had ceased its creaking and she wished for the sound. The heavy stillness was all-enveloping. She mounted the steps, one hand clutching the wooden railing, the other holding the pistol tight to her side. The feel of the gun in her hand was a comforting one now, like the touch of an old friend.

At the top of the stairwell Leah paused, peering into the gloom ahead. A corridor twisted sharply out from one side of the landing. She turned into it—and from the dark recessed corner, a bulky shape fell slowly forward.

Leah saw vacant eyes. Saw lips twisted into a macabre grimace. She felt dead flesh brush against her own skin. She screamed—and screamed again and again as the body plunged past her to thud heavily from step to step, landing finally in a contorted heap at the foot of the stairs.

Stomach churning with fear and nausea, Leah fell limply over the balustrade. The door below crashed open, the sound jerking her upright like a puppet, arms thrust out straight before her, pistol gripped in both hands. Giddy with a panic that blotted out all conscious thought, Leah pulled back hard on the trigger and fired into the shadows. The shot exploded in her head, the force of it sending her stumbling backwards. She heard the bullet splinter wood.

The smell of burning powder filled her nostrils, and through the black haze drifting slowly upwards from the barrel of her gun, Leah saw the powerful figure of Cole McCullough filling the doorway. He stood outlined against a dusky sky, knees bent, body tensed in a half crouch, Colt drawn. Deliberately he straightened and holstered his revolver.

Leah could not speak, the silence within her brain as deafening as the crack of the pistol. She could not move, her arms still held stiffly before her. She could only watch Cole come forward from the shadows with the stealthy grace of a prowling cat.

All at once her rigid body began a violent trembling. There was a curious loud roaring in her ears, the ceiling beginning to spin dizzily above her. She shut her eyes, the gun slipped from her hand, and she swayed against the wall.

Leah clenched her teeth. She would not faint—she could not! Not in front of Cole McCullough! How he would jeer at her if she went into a swoon like some wilting flower. She pressed her shoulder blades hard to the wall, willing herself to strength. The rough wooden planking pinched her spine but pierced the fog that was clouding her brain. The pounding in her ears began to subside. She blinked, discovered the world had righted itself, and opened her eyes wide to see Cole looking down at her. He stood with folded arms, one shoulder propped casually against the wall.

'I—I didn't faint,' Leah murmured with a kind of little girl pride.

'That you didn't.' His voice was dry, cool as spring water. 'But you're going to have to learn to shoot straighter. You missed me by a mile.'

One hand at her forehead, Leah tried to piece together the fragments. 'I heard the door open— It frightened me, startled me—' The thick black brows drew together in sharp puzzlement and she frowned up at him. 'Where—where did you come from?'

Cole laughed shortly. From beneath the dark moustache his lips curled back over white, even teeth. 'Where did I come from?' He lifted a hand, bracing it on the wall above her, and leaned in close. 'From hell, Miss Cabot.'

A suppressed violence in the sardonic words sent a small tremor through Leah's body. She saw flames leap in the amber eyes. But were they the flames of the inferno outside—or some private hell only he knew of?

'Leah . . .'

The voice was faint, but unmistakably familiar, and it had come from somewhere nearby. Leah whirled around. Flattening one hand against the wall to steady herself, she began groping her way down the dark corridor.

'I'm coming, Grandfather!'

A thin streak of light beckoned up from beneath a doorway at the opposite end of the hall and Leah hurried towards it. She was but dimly aware of Cole behind her—the small patch of brightness ahead had become her only reality.

Half-running, half-stumbling in her eagerness, Leah pushed through the door to find a small, square room, a candle in a smoke-smudged chimney flickering from atop a crude wooden table. Beside the table stood a low-backed cot and the wavering light fell full over the man who lay there.

A cry of joy rose in Leah's throat, but as she approached the bed, the joy died on her lips.

It could not be—this could not be Grandfather John, not the patriarch of Cabot Academy with his strong-featured face, his burning eyes. This man . . . this man's face was shrunken and pinched, his eyes sunk deep within violet shadows. Against the waxy pallor of his skin, the white mane of hair and flowing white beard seemed a ghastly jest.

'Grandfather John?'

The rising and falling of his chest beneath a red-stained bandage was barely perceptible and Leah knew a surge of cold fear. Had she come minutes too late? But no. Slowly he moved his head against the rough ticking of the pillow and looked at her.

'I—I heard you calling me, Leah . . .' The ringing tones of command had faded to a tremulous whisper. 'I heard you scream . . . the gunshot . . . You're—you're all right?'

Leah nodded quickly, words falling with fevered urgency. 'I'm fine, Grandfather, but I must fetch you the doctor—you must be tended to—'

'They've done . . . all they can for me . . .'

'No!'

It was the first time she had ever spoken against him. Dismayed, Leah clapped a hand over her mouth, yet still she whispered a frantic protest. 'There must be a way to help you, Grandfather! Some way—'

'There's nothing,' Cole's voice cut harshly. 'He's dying.'

Leah tensed, flinging brittle words at him with a vengeance. 'You have no right to say that, Mr McCullough! You—you have no right to be here!' Her voice choked on a sob and she fell to her knees, the coarse woollen blanket scratching her face as she pressed close to the bed. 'No right—no right—'

There was brief silence, and then the hollow thud of boots striking wood sounded up hard and swift and faded to nothingness.

'Leah, I will not . . . will not permit you to . . . act this way. Calm . . . yourself!'

A glimmer of the well-remembered indomitability echoed in the wasted voice and for an instant Fort Laramie, the weeks on the trail—all disappeared, and Leah was back once more in the quiet house in Boston. Back before the war, before the world had changed. She twined her arms together, gripping herself tightly. With the discipline born of long habit she lifted her head and said quietly, 'I'm sorry, Grandfather.'

The white head moved a bare fraction in a nod of satisfaction. His strength barely that of a child's, Grandfather John pressed her hand. It was the closest he had ever—would ever—come to a caress.

'You were always . . . obedient, Leah.'

He paused, fighting painfully for breath, and deep within the sunken eyes, Leah saw burning still sparks of the old iron will, embers that could not be extinguished.

She knew that it was by the sheer force of that will that Grandfather John had clung to life until she'd arrived, that it was with the force of that will alone that he was keeping death at bay now.

'Your scout . . . arrived at the Fort a few days ago . . . He said—he said you would be coming soon . . . So I knew—I knew I had only a little while . . . to wait.' He shut his eyes and the struggle for continued speech etched itself even more deeply on the ravaged face. 'On the table, Leah . . . look on the table. You must—must see . . . must know . . .'

His words held strange urgency, and bewilderedly, Leah glanced around to the wooden table to see a rose cockade lying within the circle of smokey light. Her fingers closed around the embroidered white petals, but her brain could make no sense of the trinket, nor why it was so important.

'What is this, Grandfather?'

'It . . . it was dropped in the raid—' The faint voice sharpened to a hoarse rasp. '*They—they* dropped it . . .'

Leah leaned close. 'Who dropped it, Grandfather? One of the men who attacked the Fort?'

But John Cabot was past hearing, caught in a sudden, terrible frenzy of the past. His hands began a fitful plucking at the blankets, his white head moving painfully against the pillow.

'Micah—Micah gone . . . The Academy—gone . . . All . . . all gone . . .' He licked his lips as if to make speech come easier, but when he again summoned the strength to go on, his words were even more disjointed. 'Everything . . . everything . . . gone . . . they . . . they . . . took . . . everything . . .'

Appalled, Leah stared down at him, saw the twitching

hands, heard the rasping voice. It wasn't right! It wasn't fair! That death should drive Grandfather John into this tormented delirium—John Cabot, who had based his whole life on cool logic and calm reason. She put a hand on either of his shoulders, trying to quiet him. 'Please, Grandfather,' she begged, 'please lie still—'

But the anguished phrases kept on and on, and his pitiful intent on old pain, old memories, wrung Leah's heart. Oh, it wasn't right!

The claw-like hands, contorted in pain, clutched at her arms. With demented fury Grandfather John pulled himself a few inches from the bed, his eyes opening to show his gaze blazing hot and wild. His face wore the crazed mask of a madman.

'Never—never forget! Never . . . forget—'

His grip slackened. The violence drained from his face. As quickly as it had come, the delirium left him. Gently, very gently, Leah lowered his head to the pillow.

'Thank you, God,' she murmured fervently. John Cabot would pass his final moments in sanity and peace.

Life was ebbing, but one task remained.

'Pledge, Leah . . . pledge that you will carry on . . . the dream . . .' The last vestiges of the iron will flickered in his eyes. 'Pledge . . . Leah . . .'

'I pledge, Grandfather,' she answered clearly.

John Cabot sighed softly and shut his eyes. The struggle was over.

Ever so lightly, Leah let her fingertips graze the white hair, then quickly she drew back. She squeezed her hands into fists, squeezed so hard the knuckles went white.

Grandfather John had never approved of emotional

displays. She could not break the lessons of a lifetime. Not even now. She must remain dry eyed and quiet and correct, her farewell to him as subdued as her life with him. For that was the goodbye he would have wished.

And as she knelt there, aching with unshed tears, unspent grief, a hard crust, like ice, began to form about her heart. Slowly the deadening chill spread outward, into every part of her body. Only her brain would not be still—it was filled with a single, throbbing thought.

Pledge, Leah. Pledge, Leah. Pledge, Leah.

Long ago, so very long ago, Micah had spoken those same words to her. Now his words had come again into her life, claimed her life.

The candle was guttering down in a kind of death agony of its own, casting restless shadows on walls and ceiling, and its writhings were like the windings and twistings of Leah's mind as it spiralled backward. She was flooded with memories, of her brother, of her parents. Of Grandfather John. Memories that moved in an endless procession across her mind, even as the flaring shadows moved around and around the small room.

Leah sank back on her heels, face buried in her hands. Past and present touched and became one, and the shadows and her memories surrounded her, took possession of her.

She would never know how long she remained so, mere minutes or an eternity, but finally, from somewhere far, far away, the sound of footsteps brushed the very edge of her consciousness.

'I tried to find the doctor—to bring him here. He was killed in the raid.'

Cole's voice came as if from a great distance . . . its

husky drawl fighting the nether world into which Leah had crept. As if she were moving through water, she dragged up her head. Framed by the heavy masses of burnished hair, her face wore the dazed look of a sleepwalker.

'It doesn't matter,' she said in a dull, singsongy tone. She stared fixedly at the final glimmerings of the dying candle. 'You were right. My Grandfather is dead.'

Cole walked past her to stand by the bed, looking down at the still figure for a moment. He turned. 'The fire's out and we've circled the wagons within the Fort. Leah, it's time to go.'

She tried to fathom his words. Go? Where must she go? What must she do? Grandfather John had always ordered her life, but now he lay on that rough cot in this bleak room, forever gone from her.

Pledge, Leah.

Yes, yes—the pledge. That was what she must hold to. But how? How was she to do that? Her brain felt so fuzzy and thick. Her body felt so odd, as if it were hung with manacles.

'It's time to go,' Cole said again.

Why did he keep saying that? Didn't he see that she could not move? Could not feel, could not think. That her mind and body were both as dead as Grandfather John. Why couldn't he see, why couldn't he understand?

Leah looked at him and the dark green eyes were wide with a child's bewilderment. Wordlessly Cole bent and lifted her in his arms.

She should protest. This man—this man whom she'd first seen in the night shadows and who was carrying her down the stairs and into the shadows of another night— was not to be trusted. He had told her himself he was not to be trusted. Yet she clung to him.

Cole said nothing, only carried her through the darkness, and she shut her eyes, pressing close against him. She could feel the beating of his heart, hear his heavy breathing, and these sounds and his touch filled the world, were all she wanted from the world.

His arms were hard about her and she sapped the very vitality of those arms, drew strength from his strength. She felt the unyielding power of his body flow into her, through her, shattering the chill core of ice around her heart, freeing the aching pain.

And now the tears came, trickling in twin tracks down her cheeks to fall against him, but still he said nothing, only carried her through the night.

The glowing remains of a campfire near the wagon, the coffee pot and tin cup, gave evidence that Birdie had taken a brief respite from the fire, though there was no sign of her now. Cole dropped to one knee beside the bed of embers, lifting Leah to the ground. Slowly she raised her head, the tumble of her hair grazing his cheek. For a moment she let her twined arms linger about his neck, unwilling to break the gossamer thread that had bound them.

But the eyes that met hers were like glass beads, offering nothing, asking nothing. Before their hard indifference her own glance fell, her hands dropped to her lap—and one tightly knotted fist opened to show the rose cockade.

Had she been holding it all this time? Or had it really been so long? How odd that a world could change so completely in so short a time, that a life could end in the small span between heartbeats.

'Where did you get that?'

There was a tight, almost strangled sound to Cole's words, and Leah was aware of the sudden, sharp indrawing of his body, like someone just dealt a stunning blow. Wonderingly, she fingered the white rose as she answered him.

'My grandfather found it. He said it was dropped during the raid. Do you know what it is? Have you seen it before?'

A moment passed. A muscle began twitching convulsively in Cole's face as he stared at the rose cockade—and in one swift, violent motion he wrenched it from Leah's grasp and came to his feet. He stood with legs wide apart, body tense and still. The hand that held the cockade was clenched at his side.

'It's the Cherokee Rose. And yes—I've seen it before.' His voice was toneless now, a dead thing, wiped clean of all emotion. 'I thought I'd never see it again.'

His gaze bore into her, but Leah knew he was not seeing her. His eyes were empty, blank as his voice, as if he were looking past this place, through this time. As if he were no longer looking without, but within, to some dark and bitter memory. Looking to that private hell whose flames she had glimpsed before?

'The Cherokee Rose,' Leah whispered. And was this rose, this flower plucked from a room of death, somehow linked with the hell that lay behind the amber gaze?

Purposefully, with sure, fluid grace, Leah moved to stand close before Cole. Her emotions had been pared to the raw edge in the hazy, half-world of grief and memories he had carried her from. Her fear had been stripped away. And in its place was something bold and strong. She could not play at denial now.

Whatever Cole McCullough's link with the rose cockade, she did not care. Whoever this man was, wherever he had come from, at this moment, she did not care. She cared only that the dark, lean face was drawn, set in the harsh lines of some grim remembrance. She cared only that he was in torment—and that from deep within the well of loneliness that was her life, she must find a way to fight against his pain.

Leah lifted both hands to his face. She traced a pattern over the strong curve of his jaw, over the high, ridged cheekbones, over his lips, trying to smooth away his anguish. She caressed his shoulders, trying to ease the tautness of his body with her touch. She pressed her fingertips against his chest, feeling the rapid cadence of his breathing beneath the buckskin shirt, feeling his breath on her face.

Cole turned his head slightly away, watching her warily from under half lowered lids. Then abruptly he reached out for her. With a savage tenderness he caught one hand, turning it palm up to press his lips against the pulse at her wrist. Leah felt those lips like fire against her skin, felt the beat of that pulse filling her body.

His head lifted, and the tawny eyes were naked with an emotion as powerful and unreadable as the man himself. His jaw set. The guarded mask slipped again over his face. He flung her off, as if the very touch of her seared his flesh.

And as he moved away and into the darkness, Leah heard the decisive crunch of his boots against the hard packed earth.

She smoothed her hands down the line of her body, trying to still its throbbing. She was aching with a want only half understood, filled with a desire that cried out across the darkness for relief.

But there was no answer.

Her breath was coming hard and fast, as if she had been running, and she wanted to run, into the night, after him.

But it would do no good.

She had lost him. With the sure, strange knowledge that had bound her heart to this man from the first moment she'd seen him, Leah knew that she had lost him. Lost him to that hidden, hellish place behind the tawny eyes.

Or could you lose what you had never possessed?

In the morning, Cole McCullough was gone from Fort Laramie.

CHAPTER
FOUR

'THE Lord is my shepherd: I shall not want . . .'

Alonzo Simms' heavy voice rumbled over the stillness of afternoon, but Leah found her thoughts wandering from his words. This brief service seemed but a formality. Her real goodbye to Grandfather John had been said two days past, in that small, square room, in that twilight of memories.

The civilian cemetery topped a small rise directly opposite the Fort. A lone cottonwood stood in the centre of the clearing and brown prairie grass grew long between the headstones. Two new graves had been dug just that morning.

John Cabot and Jeremy Fisher. Eastern scholar and western mountain man, both felled in the renegade attack. Their lives had taken different routes, but both paths had converged and ended within the adobe walls of Fort Laramie.

'He restoreth my soul: he leadeth me in the paths of righteousness for his name's sake . . .'

How hot it was. Leah could feel the damp clinging of her petticoat against her legs, and beneath the high-necked bodice a trickle of perspiration ran between her breasts. The lace veil on her bonnet was like a warm breath across her face.

The last of her Boston clothes. They'd been long since

packed away, but it had seemed only fitting that she wear them for this one afternoon. Only proper.

Propriety. Once it had been the cornerstone of her life. She had given it scant thought these months on the trail, but all that would change now.

'Thou preparest a table before me in the presence of mine enemies . . .'

Yes, from now on she would be as proper as she had been in Boston. As obedient to those rules that had once governed her life. She would have no reason not to be. Cole McCullough was gone.

He was gone—and the searing need of two nights ago had become a dull ache, steady as her heartbeat, merciless as the glare of the sun.

He was gone—and as on that first morning, Leah found herself asking the same question, over and over.

Had she really expected him to stay?

'Surely goodness and mercy shall follow me all the days of my life: and I will dwell in the house of the Lord forever. Amen.'

The wagonmaster looked up. 'That does it for the buryin', folks.' He shut the worn black Bible with a thump. 'But now I got me somethin' to say, and this seems as good a time as any to say it. I don't mean no disrespect for the dead—Jeremy Fisher and me travelled a lot of miles together. But on the trail it's the livin' you got to think of.'

Simms bent to retrieve his sombrero, straightening slowly, and there was unusual restraint in his manner as he stood twisting his hat in his hands. 'I'll put it to you plain,' he began finally, ''cause I don't know any other way. This train's at a bad pass. Our scout's gone and we ain't been able to scrape up but half of the supplies I was countin' on. But the worst of it is—somewheres between us and the mountains is a whole passel of riled up Sioux and Cheyenne.'

A sharp ripple moved over the gathering. The men shifted on their feet, the women looked to one another. Sudden fear punctured the hush of afternoon.

'Why don't we try tradin' with them Injuns?' Birdie called out above the crowd, standing flat footed and firm beside Leah. 'It worked with the Pawnee!'

'We ain't broken no treaties with the Pawnee!' Simms responded with emphasis. 'The Sioux and Cheyenne have had a bellyfull of false promises. They're just itchin' to get back a little of their own! With that pack of white renegades supplyin' 'em guns and ammunition and God knows what, they ain't in no mood for a pow-wow!'

Caleb Rance elbowed forward, a short, squat, bow-legged man in the red flannel shirt and kneeboots of the miner. 'Can't we get some help from the soldiers here? The government told us that after the war the trail West would be safe again!'

Simms shook his head. 'This garrison has lost too many men already to send a patrol with us. We'll just have to take our chances alone.'

'You think we oughtta be willin' to take our chances with you, Simms?' Eb Hutter's words fell with strident disrespect. 'Seein' as how you already made one mistake.'

Digging the toe of one boot in the dirt, his face expressionless, the wagonmaster considered the tall, rawboned man before him.

'Don't rightly know what mistake you mean.'

'Don't you?' Hutter demanded insolently. With measured deliberation he ran his hands beneath his suspenders, a hard expression on his beaked face. 'I mean hirin' Cole McCullough!'

Leah drew up so sharply she caught Birdie's eye. She steadied herself, but a strange apprehension began circling, snakelike, in the pit of her stomach.

'You're the one hired that damn drifter as an outrider, Simms,' Hutter went on sullenly, 'and now—jest when we need him the most—he up and disappears!'

'Why don't you mind your own business, Hutter!' Sourdough O'Rourke spat out contemptuously.

Bristling like a banty rooster, Sourdough elbowed his way through the crowd. He stepped close to the rangy homesteader, settled his hands on his hips and jutted out his chin. 'I'm gettin' mighty tired of your flappin' lip, Hutter!'

With a venomous oath, Eb Hutter spun his loose-limbed body about like a willow switch and charged for the fiddler. But though the man topped him by a foot, Sourdough didn't flinch. Flipping the cigar from his mouth, he lifted his fists.

'Come on, Hutter,' Sourdough baited him, jabbing away with energy if without effect, 'I'm gonna cut you down to size!'

'Keep your left up, Sourdough!' Birdie called out encouragingly, demonstrating a few punches of her own. She whooped in delight. 'I sure do like me a scrappy man!'

Burly as a bear, the wagonmaster waded into the crowd. He jammed on his sombrero, then spread his hands wide to catch both Hutter and Sourdough by their shirtfronts and pulled them up short.

'Simmer down, the both of ya!'

The opponents eyed each other like a pair of surly

gamecocks, but under the wagonmaster's relentless grip
they finally dropped their eyes and lowered their fists.
Satisfied, Simms nodded once, releasing the men as if
they were sacks of grain. He pivoted to face the others.

'I admit I was wrong in hirin' McCullough,' Simms
began, 'but I always figured a man was entitled to one
mistake.' He paused, a flinty edge lurking just below the
deceptively mild surface as he faced them all down.
Carefully he brushed the back of one hand across his big
jaw. 'But if any of you have doubts—'bout me or what we
might be facin'—you can pull out and head back East
and there'll be no questions asked. But know this—' The
wagonmaster shot a glance around the semi-circle of
upturned faces that took the measure of every man and
woman there. 'Once we leave here we hit the Rockies
and then the desert, and then the special hell of the
Sierra Nevadas. After Fort Laramie there's no turnin'
back. Not for any of us.'

Without another word Simms wheeled down the
slope. Silent now, subdued, the others followed, but
Leah pushed against the crowd, up the hill.

No turning back . . . Alonzo Simms' words had struck
a hollow note within her, mirroring Birdie's question to
her the day after the fire.

'Child—' the cracked voice had held uncharacteristic
hesitation, 'I'm powerful sorry 'bout yer Grandpa, and I
reckon his dyin' has started you to wonderin' some,
'bout keepin' on, I mean. Now I know the wagon and all
the supplies he bought went up in the fire—' She'd
stopped suddenly and banged an impatient fist against
her thigh. 'Aw shoot! I never was one to pussyfoot
around! What I'm tryin' to say is, we've been gettin' on
like a regular pair of matched mules and I'd be mighty

pleased to have you with me the rest of the way to California! So I'm askin' you plain—are you goin' on or turnin' back?'

There had been only one answer. She had made her pledge.

Grandfather John was gone, but in his dying he had left her with no less than what she'd always had. The Cabot dream. Fate had played the cruellest trick of all, leaving that dream solely in her hands. But she would see to the fulfillment of it. She had nothing else. Cole McCullough was gone.

Fighting reason, fighting sanity—feeling a hope stronger than both—Leah swung suddenly around. She threw back her veil and lifted her eyes to the horizon, straining for the sight of a horseman. And knowing even as she did so that the search was a futile one.

He would not return.

All that was left to her of Cole McCullough was the memory of those moments his life had touched her own. Memories bittersweet and hot as flame, that burnt to her very soul.

Turn back? Leah Cabot had nothing to turn back to. No more than she had ahead. A borrowed dream—and the ashes of remembrance.

Slowly Leah started down the hill.

The wagons pushed forward the next morning, on into the foothills of the Rockies. The trail tilted steadily upwards now, over a broken land of rock and sand, greasewood and sage.

They rode armed. While the women held the reins, their menfolk sat beside them, Winchesters or long barrelled Sharps cradled close. Simms ordered the wagons into two protective parallel lines during the day. At night they drew the circle tight and doubled the guard.

And day and night, men and women alike searched the horizon.

Around the edge of that steepsided gorge? Behind the curve of that canyon wall? Was that where the line of redskinned warriors and renegade whites would appear? Maybe not. But they were out there—somewhere.

Eight days out of Fort Laramie found them in the shadow of a great table rock that swept long and high over the surrounding countryside. The trail had left the river, forcing them to make camp near a small backwater that lay between two bluffs, its banks completely encircled with heavy brush.

The evening meal eaten and cleared, the women had gathered with their soiled clothes at the water's edge, the towering, red-faced Mrs Rance keeping watch with levelled rifle.

They worked quickly, jerking their clothes through the water with nervous hands, voices muted. More than once they glanced to the brush—suspecting every sound, hearing danger in every snap of a twig. Remembering the wagonmaster's warning:

'When you see an Indian, worry. When you *don't* see an Indian, worry twice as much.'

Alonzo Simms had warned them as well never to stray alone from the wagons and so, scrubbing done, they moved together towards the camp, Emma Rance leading the way with an ominous tread intended to warn away any assailants.

Still on her knees, Leah watched the others disappear through the dense thicket. Knowing she must not stay, prompting herself to rise yet she lingered on, hugging the moment.

It felt so good to be alone, completely alone. She sighed softly, letting the silence steal over her. Nothing of the past was hidden here, nor the future, nothing to remind her of anything.

Or anyone.

There was only the lazy drone of insects, the mouldering, pungent smell of wet ground, the lazy lapping of the water. It was the very emptiness of this glade that held comfort.

But she must go. To remain any longer would be foolish. Reluctantly Leah stood and lifted her basket of clothes.

Softer than the wind, a slight movement danced the leaves of the cottonwoods. Slowly, uneasily, Leah backed up the slope, scanning the opposite bank and beyond. She saw the brown hump of hills, saw the broad gash of a ravine—saw this and nothing else. The line of brush and bluff held still. But did that very stillness hold menace?

Leah dropped the basket, spun around, and began to run.

A shadow fell across her path. Her head lifted, and in that split second, Leah read her fate in the gleaming, coppery face before her.

Something struck hard against the side of her skull, a dazzling brightness flashed before her eyes. And as she plunged into oblivion, her last thoughts were of the man she had no hope for, his name her wordless, despairing plea. *Cole . . .*

There had never been such darkness.

Like a living thing it pressed against Leah's body,

crushing her within its thick, black folds. Her heart seemed held in an iron fist, a fist of fear, that tightened its grip with the passing of every dark and silent second . . .

Shuddering, Leah turned her head against the cave wall, feeling its cold clamminess on her cheek. Desperately she sought to sort through the blur of bewilderment.

There had been a sense of deep peacefulness, spinning suddenly into blinding pain. The world had dissolved, reappearing as a whirling mesh of tree and sky and hoofbeats.

The motion had ceased, she'd been carried deep within the earth . . . and the blackness had closed around her. Buried her.

Perhaps she had been buried alive.

Perhaps this dark, dank hole was to be her tomb for all eternity.

Leah's heart began a heavy thudding, the beats pounding louder and louder, without and within, until they filled body and brain. Until they filled the darkness and the silence. Until she thought she would go mad.

A noise without, like stones rolling one over the other, scraped against her inner frenzy, quelling it. Leah caught her breath, this sudden sound charged with greater terror than even the stillness.

The tiny cavity flared with light. Blinking against the brightness, Leah saw an Indian crawl into the chamber, torch held in one hand. He was bare to the waist, a tomahawk stuck in the belt of his deerskin leggings, and from his feathered topknot, braids fell to his shoulders.

As the gleaming, coppery face drew close, Leah gasped in recognition of her captor. Eyes dilated and near numb with fright, she shrank back against the wall, lifting her bound hands as if to ward him off. Impatiently the brave seized her arm and dragged her from the cell, Leah wincing as the jagged rocks tore through her skirt to cut at her legs.

Once into the passageway, the Indian yanked her to her feet, then gave her a violent shove that sent her staggering forward. With shaking legs, Leah started into the darkness ahead.

The torch cast a contorted shadow on the rock-whorled corridor, a following shadow that moved as Leah moved, turned as she turned. Intersecting passages twisted up with heart stopping suddenness, only to fall away into nothingness, but the looming shadow behind showed no hesitation. Onward Leah went.

The ceiling dropped abruptly, forcing her to bend double, then lifted again to reveal a circular chamber topped by an upside-down forest of stalactites. Like a frozen waterfall, layers of rock cascaded down the walls to a floor that sloped precariously, dipping cuplike in the centre.

The air was heavy with smoke, fetid with the reek of cheap whiskey. Torches hung in wall brackets lit the cavernous chamber with isolated pockets of light, showing up the figures of armed men. Some sat sprawled in crude wooden chairs, bottles in their hands, others leaned carelessly against the rock-ribboned walls, cigarettes dangling from their lips. They wore a rough mixture of deerskin and homespun, with here and there a piece of army garb, forage cap or brassbuttoned tunic, adding a bizarre finishing touch.

Needles of terror tingled along Leah's spine, up her legs, down her arms. As if she had fallen hard from some high place, her breath left her body in a sickening

rush. Soon, soon she must awaken from this nightmare.

But this was no dream and there would be no escape.
She'd been ushered to the very vestibule of hell itself—
and these silent, staring men were the leering gargoyles
who would welcome her into the flames.

A long table hung mistily in the farthest shadows, all
but the hazy outlines of the two men seated there
obscured in the surrounding gloom. One of the men
stood.

'So this is the prize you plucked from the wagon train,
Screaming Eagle.'

The voice floated up almost disembodied, arrogant
and strangely hollow of tone, slurred with a southern
accent. A voice that was somehow oddly familiar—

'I ought to reprimand you, Screaming Eagle,' the
voice continued, 'your captive does present certain—
problems. But since we've been so long without female
companionship, I won't punish you. You may go, and
tell your braves to be ready for inspection in a few
minutes.'

The Indian turned and left and the man who had
spoken came slowly forward. Emerging from the greyness of indistinction, he revealed himself as tall and slim,
clad in an immaculate white linen shirt, well-cut riding
breeches, high polished boots. Stark against his dandy's
garb, a bull whip was coiled about one shoulder.

He came closer, moving with haughty bearing, to
graze Leah with eyes so cold they seemed colourless,
pale as his silvery hair. But flickering in their depths was
a dark light, black as the lash that rested with such
chilling incongruity against the fine white shirt. His
chiselled face was marked by a scar that ran from

forehead to right cheek, ending at the corner of his mouth and twisting his thin lips into a perpetual sneer.

Leah felt her blood run cold.

For if this was hell, then surely the man who stood before her, silent, motionless save for one hand tapping a relentless tattoo against the coiled lash, was Satan.

With palpable effort Leah found words, but they were broken things, barely above a whisper. 'Who—are you? Why—why have you brought me here?'

The man snapped into a bow of practised gallantry, sweeping the room with an airy hand. 'Colonel Pierce Greville, ma'am. My men. And as for why you're here—' He set a hand beneath her chin, lifting her face to the light, and at his touch, Leah blanched. A small, almost soundless moan escaped her lips.

'As for why you're here,' Greville said again, turning her head this way and that, absorbed in idle contemplation, 'that all remains to be seen.' He smiled, twisted lips curling upwards with lurking insinuation. 'Yes, ma'am, that all remains to be seen.'

Greville stepped back, studying the lissom figure before him with a practised, impartial eye. Casually he called over his shoulder to the man at the table.

'You've always been a good judge of horseflesh—and women. What do you think of this one? Was she worth the trouble?'

Purposefully, the second man came forward—and now Leah knew this was a dream.

A dream she'd had night after night, over and over, a dream of desire and disappointment, a dream of longing and loss.

A dream of a dark, powerful man in buckskin coming towards her from the shadows.

But this time Cole McCullough did not disappear into the cold, lonely light of morning. This time he was real.

CHAPTER
FIVE

DISBELIEF broke over Leah's face, a cry of joy caught in her throat. Eagerly she started forward.

But the indifference in the tawny eyes halted her midstep.

Lazily, Cole looked her up and down, and it was the gaze of a stranger that regarded her, cool and uninterested.

'I'd say she was a rare prize.'

'Would you?' Greville frowned. 'I'll admit she has a certain gracefulness. And that hair—' He made a low sound of admiration, lifting a few strands of the chestnut mass. 'I'd hate to see that hanging on Screaming Eagle's belt. But I seem to remember you preferring the flashier type, McCullough.'

'Maybe I've come to appreciate the—virtues—of a lady.'

Cole's sardonic words were like a slap.

The hurt in Leah hardened into anger. She swept up her chin, shook back the dishevelled hair, her face flaming into defiant vividness. With level directness she returned Cole McCullough's insolent stare, and her voice was low and clear and scornful as she answered him.

'I find it hard to believe that a man like you would know much of a real lady!'

Greville lifted an eyebrow. 'Spirited filly.'

Slender fingertips began again that nervous gesture against the coiled black lash, the Colonel's smooth expression altering subtly, ominously. He shot out one hand, and in a single, deadly movement tore Leah's blouse nearly from neck to waist. Colourless eyes danced with dark lights as he glanced casually at the swell of small rounded breasts rising whitely from her chemise.

'But like a fine thoroughbred, my dear,' Greville continued in a controlled, passionless voice, 'you must learn who is the master.'

Gasping, Leah fell back a pace, clutching her bound hands over the ragged ends of her blouse. Instinctively she looked to Cole, something akin to pleading in her eyes. Bruised and violated she stood before him, ashen with shock and trembling with shame. His eyes narrowed, a corner of his mouth twitched once, but he made no move to help her.

Leah lowered her head, the heavy hair falling across her bare shoulders. The last vestige of hope shattered within her, the broken shards piercing her to the heart.

The thickset shadow of a man moved suddenly from the wall. Fired by the pent-up greediness of woman-starved lust, the man lunged at Leah with animal-like ferocity. She felt rough hands at her waist, felt foul breath hot on her face. Writhing frantically, she was borne off her feet.

To the accompaniment of catcalls and howls of laughter, the man dropped into a chair and bent Leah backwards over his knees. He pressed thick greasy lips against her throat, her shoulders. He plunged one hand beneath her chemise, pawing at her breasts.

Revulsion such as she had never known swept Leah into near insanity. She struggled madly, kicking and screaming. Wresting one hand from his grip, she seized a hank of the man's hair and pulled up hard against his scalp. Yet still he held her, still his hands fumbled over her flesh.

Then suddenly she was free.

Dazedly Leah slipped to her knees to see Cole Mc-Cullough with a hand hard about the man's throat, his muscular arm stretched out long to thrust the man's head back against the chair.

'The girl's mine,' Cole asserted tersely, tightening his grip. 'Do you understand?'

Receiving a choking assent, Cole released his hold, watching coolly as the man crumbled to the floor in a gasping heap. He lifted his head, sweeping a defiant gaze over the rest of the men. 'The girl's mine,' Cole repeated.

'Such a display of temper!'

The hollow tapping of a slender hand against coiled lash echoed up as a curious companion to Greville's acid words.

'You not only look like a frontiersman, McCullough, you behave like one. My, my, these past years have certainly changed you.'

Cole's lips tightened. 'And you, Greville.'

The Colonel's thin body jerked convulsively. The amusement drained from the chiselled face, something unfathomable rippling over the jewel-hard features that made Leah's flesh crawl.

'Nothing has changed,' Greville ground out between clenched teeth. 'Nothing!' He spun on his heel, gathering up cape and gauntlets and wide-brimmed hat from a nearby chair. With a quick, nervous gesture he flung the mantle over one shoulder.

'Gentlemen!' Greville lifted a hand over his head as if signalling a cavalry charge. 'Inspection!'

Indolently the men moved from the shadows, and Leah could feel their eyes on her, hot and piercing, as they passed. Eyes that tore through her tattered garments and stripped her bare. If one of them—just one—should break rank, she knew they would all follow, descending on her like a pack of wolves.

But the man in buckskin stood over her as he might a precious trophy, one hand on his hip, the other on his revolver. And though Greville's men mumbled harsh words among themselves, none of them ventured forth to meet the unspoken challenge in that cool amber gaze.

Pulling on fringed gauntlets, the Colonel watched the last of his band leave the chamber with an impatient eye. He bent a final, careless glance on Cole. 'Enjoy her, McCullough.'

Greville turned, the black folds of his cape melting into the darkness beyond. Cole and Leah were alone.

For a moment there was perceptible silence, a silence so keen it seemed to Leah that neither of them drew a breath.

'Leah—'

His voice sent a shaft of liquid fire running through her veins. Did it hold a note she'd never heard before, something nearly like tenderness? No. Determinedly Leah pushed the thought away, certain that it had been born of her own desperate want.

Yet the sudden touch of his hand as he knelt beside her held unwonted gentleness.

He ran his fingers beneath her hair, then slid them up

to her temples. His grip tightened and holding firm the finely cut line of her profile, he lifted her face to his, his lips hovering over hers like a breath.

Leah's own lips parted with the joy of his touch, the wonder of the moment, and the still darkness wrapped about them like a dream.

'What luck,' Cole said softly, 'to have you—like this—'

Something in his words made Leah's heart beat faster.

She drew a quick, harsh breath, rallying grimly, and summoned a rush of memory to combat the traitorous stirrings of her body. She shut her eyes, letting the moments run by her, letting the images form in her mind.

A man emerging from the shadows, knife in his hand. A man appearing as if from nowhere, framed against a dusky sky, gun drawn. The rose cockade.

'That morning, by the spring,' Leah began, voice halting and husky with strain, 'you told me you were the wrong man to trust—' She paused, and the green eyes she opened to him were tortured. 'And now I know the truth of those words.'

Leah stumbled to her feet to whisper words of incredulous fury. 'You're one of them! You came to the wagon train deliberately, to lead us into a trap! And at the Fort—in the officers' barracks—you were trying to finish what the others had started! Yes, you're one of them, one of the men who killed my grandfather—'

With trembling intent, Leah lifted her fettered hands to him. 'You've treated me tonight no better than any of your fellow renegades, Cole McCullough! Bound and unwilling—that's the only way you'll ever have me!'

The tawny eyes darkened. His mouth went curiously rigid. He stepped quickly forward, and for one terrifying instant, Leah thought he meant to strike her.

Abruptly Cole drew the knife at his belt. With a single hard slash he sliced her bonds in two. He flung the blade to the ground and, catching Leah's bare arms above the elbow, pulled her close.

'I'm no member of this band! I'm no renegade!' He began shaking her, as if to punctuate his own furious words, her head snapping back and forth on the slender column of her neck. 'Do you understand that? I'm no member of this band! I had nothing to do with the attack on the Fort! By God, I haven't sunk that low yet!'

As suddenly as he had seized her, Cole released her.

Leah reeled backwards, falling against the table, and for a space she stood so, body bent, arms aching where his fingers had cut into her flesh. Slowly she pushed the blinding mass of hair from her face to see Cole pour out a drink from the half-empty whiskey bottle that stood on the table.

'I treated you the way I did just now,' he began hoarsely, voice shaking with suppressed emotion, 'for your own good. Greville and his men have no idea that I rode with the wagon train. I had to pretend to go along with their game. If I'm going to help you—help you get away from here—it was the only way. Don't you see? If they'd realised that I knew you—'

He broke off. Wrist stiff, Cole tossed down the contents of his glass in one neat motion, and when he spoke again, his words were low but controlled.

'On the day of the fire I'd been going from building to building, trying to flush out any of the raiders that might still have been within the Fort. I went to the officers' barracks because I heard your screams. That night I left to track down the renegade camp. I found it—I came here only yesterday.'

Whiskey in one hand, glass in the other, Cole poured out another drink and bolted it.

For a brief flashing moment there had been a crack in his armour of hard imperturbability, but as he lowered the glass, Leah saw that the break had already mended. The cool lynx-like look had returned to his face.

Yet there was a new haggardness there as well.

His gaunt cheeks were shadowed with a stubble of beard, deep lines ran from nose to mouth. The tough, hard body seemed now a shade too thin, too taut.

Leah pressed her fingertips to her temples. A hundred elusive thoughts were racing through her brain, begging for an answer. And of all the pieces of this terrifying puzzle, over and above the unknowns of this renegade band, over and above Colonel Pierce Greville with his dancing master manners and his flashes of satanic rage, over and above it all, was the mystery of the man before her. Somehow she must pound the tangled threads into cohesiveness.

She drew up tightly, coming to stand with slender determination in the small circle of torchlight, and her voice fell with a quiet carefulness.

'You say that you are no part of this band, that you came here but a day ago. Yet Greville spoke of having known you before.'

'Pierce Greville was my commanding officer during the war.' Cole replaced bottle and glass with a hard thump, meeting Leah's eyes unflinchingly down the long length of the table. 'Captain Cole McCullough at your service, ma'am. Third Georgia Cavalry, Confederate States of America.'

Leah recoiled as if she'd been struck.

One hand pressed to the base of her throat, she stared at him. 'But you told Eb Hutter—you told us all—that at the surrender—'

'At the surrender I was over a thousand miles from the South,' Cole finished for her smoothly. 'Out West, in the New Mexico Territory to be exact.'

Out West . . . Now Leah understood why Colonel Greville's hard, haughty voice had evoked latent remembrance. For it was a voice like, and unlike, Cole McCullough's, Cole's words softened and lulled by a Western drawl.

One part of the puzzle had fallen jarringly into place but it had dislodged another fragment as it did so, prodding Leah's mind to a new and terrible thought. The black brows swept up like raven's wings against her white skin, the quiet question torn from her against her will.

'You—deserted?'

Cole lifted one foot to a chair, resting folded arms on his bent knee, and the amber eyes gleamed with bright malicious mockery. 'Thank you for your high opinion of me, Miss Cabot.' He shrugged. 'Maybe I did desert, maybe I didn't. What does it matter now? All the men of the Third Georgia are dead—' something flickered behind his gaze and disappeared, 'one way or another.'

'Then—these aren't the men of your regiment?'

'Lord, no!'

Cole straightened with a violence that sent the chair crashing to the floor. He tightened his hands into fists and Leah heard him draw a ragged breath, saw the heavy shoulders move tautly beneath the buckskin. He was fighting for control.

What dark anger lay caged within Cole McCullough, Leah wondered suddenly. What would be the consequences if that black rage ever broke through those self-imposed bonds?

He went on in words deadly still.

'These ruffians Greville has gathered together are the very dregs of the Southern army, border guerillas, marauders. Men who fought without official sanction, who used the war as an excuse for thievery and looting. The men I commanded—'

He broke off, swinging half-way around. 'My men,' he began again, and this time his voice was warm, rich and vibrant in a way Leah had never heard before, 'were fine and proud, all of them, with fine, proud traditions.'

His head lifted, the tenseness seeming to fall from his body, the wariness from the hard cut profile. He was no longer guarded, but open and hopeful—proud as his words about those long dead comrades. And listening to him, Leah barely breathed. She felt so close—so close to the enigma that was Cole McCullough.

'I saw those men subsist for months on starvation rations. I saw them white with pain and yellow with malaria because we had no quinine, no chloroform, no medicine. I saw them on forced marches through the Virginia winter, their feet wrapped in rags because they had no boots. I saw their bloodied tracks in the snow. I saw them sick and hungry and shabby and exhausted, but always, always they were fine and proud and gallant—'

He stopped and the light drained from his face, leaving it bleak as a windswept winter morning, and there was a look in his eyes deeper than pain. He leaned over the table, gripping the wooden planking in either hand,

and Leah saw his knuckles go white.

'The Cherokee Rose was the emblem of the Third Georgia Cavalry. Greville must have been wearing it the day he led the attack on the Fort. When you showed it to me I had to know, I had to find out if any of my men had been involved in the raid.' He closed his eyes, opening them again with effort. 'But what I came to find no longer exists.'

As if it were a long hard task, Cole straightened. Wordlessly he reached beneath the buckskin shirt and drew out the rose cockade. He tossed it on the table.

'No, there's no one here from my regiment. Pierce Greville—he's not the man I remember. He was always an arrogant devil, puffed up with pride about his plantation, his Southern heritage. But now it's as if the war— the defeat—has turned that pride into poison. Something snapped in Greville the day Lee surrendered, anything that was good in him died at Appomattox. This—is just the shell.'

Cole laughed shortly, mirthlessly. 'But maybe he's the lucky one. He's deluded himself into thinking this band of cut-throats are gallant officers of the Confederacy, that their raids and robberies are glorious victories for the South. He's dropped a veil over his eyes, he doesn't know that the war's over and the world's changed. That everything's gone.'

Everything gone.

The spectre of remembrance rose in Leah's mind.

She had heard those words before, spoken by another man in another grim and lonely place. Who had it been? Where had it been? She fumbled for the memory.

Of course. Grandfather John. What had he said?

Micah gone. The Academy gone. Everything gone.
They took everything—

The gleam of something white caught Leah's eye, and
the sight of the rose cockade took her suddenly back to a
fire-swept night, a night of death. She heard again that
hoarse, rasping voice, she saw again that pain-racked
face, crazed with delirium, wild with some strange
urgency, pleading with her to listen—to look at a white
rose lying in a circle of smokey candlelight.

'It . . . it was dropped in the raid—*They*—*they* dropped it . . .'

The light of realisation hit Leah with physical force.
She clutched at the table with both hands to keep from
falling.

Grandfather John had known—he'd known—that the
rose cockade was a Confederate symbol. His madness
had been no torment of the past, but a desperate need of
the present. He'd wanted her to understand that those
same men whose war had taken Cabot Academy, whose
bullets had taken Micah—those men had taken his life as
well.

He'd wanted her to understand, and he'd wanted her
to remember. In the last minutes of his life, with his last
remnants of strength, John Cabot had gasped out to her
that final directive.

Never forget.

Never forget that it was the Confederate dream of
rebellion that had ended his life, ended his dream, left
her the sole heir of the Cabot legacy.

Leah stared at the white rose, stared unblinking until
her eyes grew watery and the petals wavered and dissolved and gave way to the sight of a dark, hard-muscled
man in a grey uniform. A man with Captain's epaulettes

on his shoulders and his sabre drawn. A man riding to war against her brother, her people. Against all the tenets of her life.

Quicker than conscious thought, moving at the impetus of orders drilled into her deeper even than her own desires, Leah seized the rose cockade. As if flinging down a gauntlet, she hurled it to the floor between them. Swiftly she lifted her head and clasped her hands behind her back, her jaw tightened to unaccustomed hardness, her green eyes went emerald.

'The North lost in the war as well as the South, Mr McCullough. We lost fine, proud men, too—young men. We lost homes and property. Some of us lost a way of life.'

The strength of her own voice surprised Leah, stiffened her spine, goaded her on.

'And may I remind you that it was the South who fired the first shot, who began the first battle. It was your Confederacy that wanted a war. Well—' She drew a long, triumphant breath. 'We gave you one you'll not soon forget!'

Hollow laughter crashed from Cole's throat, laughter so unexpected in the tense, grey silence, Leah started.

'The proper Miss Leah Cabot of Boston,' white teeth showed beneath the dark moustache as Cole caressed the words with gibing relish. 'A regular red-hot little Yankee. No doubt you're chastising yourself right now for the way you once helped a Confederate soldier.'

At the taunting words that so neatly echoed her own thoughts, Leah went crimson. Grinning at her discomfort, Cole came deliberately forward.

'But Confederate though I am, Miss Cabot, I am also your only protection against that rabble outside.'

The traces of a honeyed drawl still clung to his husky voice, to his idle words, but now there was something else, too, a maliciousness more forbidding than anger. And as he hovered over her, so close she could feel the heat of his body through her clothes, to her skin and deeper, Leah knew the heady fear of a cornered animal.

'Instead of hurling insults at me,' Cole went on softly, insinuatingly, lifting a hand to lightly graze her shoulders, her breasts, 'you should be begging my pardon.'

His touch left her weak with a welling, melting warmth that seemed to turn her very bones to water. But not as the rising tide within, were the thoughts that settled her brain. She flared with a wild confused anger, anger at a war not of her own making, anger at a world rent in two by that war and left forever changed. Anger at the man before her and all he represented.

But most of all there was anger at her own treacherous body. For even now—even here—Cole McCullough drew her like a moth to a flame.

Desperately Leah called on that anger to fight her feelings, fight her own soul, to shake off the years and generations of quiet Bostonians and summon forth the mettle Jeremiah Cabot had used to conquer a new world. She flung back her head, feeling that raw courage flood her veins.

'Your threats don't frighten me, Cole McCullough! I have no intention of begging anything from a traitorous southern rebel!'

Cole's body stilled, his hands balled into hard fists. He swung suddenly away, face hidden, his shadow looming large on the wall behind him.

'I've claimed you twice as my woman, Miss Cabot, the last time at considerable danger to myself. I think it's time to see if you were worth the effort.'

He did not lift his voice, neither did he stress his word
in any way, but their meaning flailed like a whip. Leah
stood rooted. The pit of her stomach dropped away, and
she went hot and cold, shivery with a strange antici-
patory excitement.

Then all at once she bolted, making a desperate bid
for freedom. But was it Cole McCullough she was
escaping from—or herself?

With tread as swift and light as a mountain lion's, Cole
was beside her. Roughly he pinned her against the wall,
caressing her shoulders with brutal intent.

'You little fool,' he murmured, and his eyes gleamed
cat yellow, 'there's no way out.'

Cole slid one hand down her arm, seizing her wrist in a
grip so savage Leah cried out in pain. But if he heard her
he did not care. He dragged her deep into the shadows of
the cavernous room, to where a flare of yellow lantern
light spread out from a natural recess cut deep in the
wall.

With a snap of his arm, Cole flung Leah forward. She
threw out her hands, bracing herself for a fall, and her
fingers touched cold metal. Quickly she pushed away,
eyes going wide with horrified amazement. Packed close
in the rocky cleft was a glittering armoury of weapons,
sabres and bayonets, pistols and carbines, powder kegs
and ammunition belts. All of it United States Army
issue, all of it taken, Leah realised, from Fort Laramie,
lifted from dead men, looted from burning buildings.

There were other treasures piled helter-skelter in the
chasm as well, strongboxes, barrels, sacks, chests. All of
it purchased at the point of a gun, all of it ransomed in
blood.

Leah averted her eyes. She could look no more, her mind shrinking away from the image this booty evoked, the remembered sight of still bodies lining a dusty quadrangle.

'Greville's band has had a busy time of it,' Cole observed wryly.

Leah turned on him like a small fury.

'Where is your pity?' she demanded hoarsely. 'Don't you realise how many innocent people Greville and his men must have murdered to secure these things?'

A corner of Cole's mouth slanted violently downward. 'Pity died in me a long time ago.'

Leah looked him full in the face, and both anger and outrage were gone from the dark green eyes, leaving them stark with simple honesty.

'Then I feel very sorry for you,' she said with quiet vehemence, and her soft words were laced with a contempt that struck like a blow.

Cole went pale beneath his tan, face twitching. For a rare moment triumph burned in Leah's breast. She had wounded him and she was glad.

Abruptly Cole strode past her. With a fierce lunge he kicked open a heavy oaken chest.

'There should be something in there.'

His voice was masked, his dark face impassive. He went, impatiently rifling through the contents of the bullet-scarred coffer, and a welter of garments poured forth. Shawls and hats and gloves and petticoats and fans. And dresses, a bewildering profusion of dresses, organdies and lawns and woollen merinos, sprigged muslins, heavy velvets, rich taffetas. Like butterflies, caught and caged and suddenly freed, the colours spilled into the murky greyness, bottle green and silver, bright blue and deep plum, red plaids, crimson stripes.

But it was none of these fulsome creations that Col
chose. He drew out a gown of the finest white silk
perfectly plain, adorned with neither ruffle nor flounce
and flung it at her.

'Put it on,' he ordered her briefly, 'you look like
homesteader's wife in what you're wearing, and I'v
never fancied pioneer woman.'

For the space of a dozen heartbeats Leah stood lik
one frozen, the dress held fast in her near numb grasp, i
silken folds swirling about her body like morning mist.

'You don't mean—'

Cole laughed on a note of savage relish. 'Oh, but I d
mean.'

He settled back in a chair, stretched out his boote
legs before him and folded his arms across his heav
chest. He settled the slouch felt hat low on his forehead
and from beneath the brim, the amber eyes raked he
with glittering amusement. 'And stand closer to the ligh
while you undress. I'd like to give my property
thorough inspection.'

Leah went chalk white, black brows and green eye
etched with haunting vividness against her pale face
The gown slipped from her hands.

Didn't he know what this would cost her, a girl raise
as she had been raised, didn't he know how this woul
shame her, abase her?

But of course he knew.

Through lips stiff with shock, Leah managed a barel
formed whisper. 'Have you no mercy?'

Cole lifted an eyebrow, and his voice held cool satis
faction.

'Are you begging me, Miss Cabot?'

Something in Leah broke in two.

Something that was neither anger nor pride but stronger than both, welled within her.

If Cole McCullough thought that by stripping away his final defence he would defeat her, she must—she must—prove him wrong. With a quiet gesture that yet held steel, Leah lifted her head. Slowly she slipped the torn blouse from her shoulders. She undid her skirt, letting it slide from her hips.

Clad only in chemise and pantalettes, Leah stepped into the arc of the light. Defiantly she let the mellow glow of the lantern outline her slender figure. Cole's face was a thing of shadowed hollows, his expression hidden, but she heard him catch a sharpened breath—and a strange exultation sang through her senses.

With an unhurried gesture, Leah lifted the white gown and slid it over her head, revelling in the feel of the fine silk against her skin. Without benefit of petticoat or hoop, the dress clung to her body, falling in severe, simple lines that served only to accent the gracefulness of her figure. From the low-cut bodice her throat and shoulders rose like ivory, the burnished lustre of her hair a single, hectic touch of colour.

Like a rare white flower on a slender stem, Leah swayed lightly before Cole McCullough. And as she stood so, the mantle of her modesty fallen away, she was conscious as never before—perhaps for the first time in her life—of her own womanliness, of her own desirability.

Slowly Cole uncoiled his powerful body from the chair. He stepped close. Deliberately he let his eyes travel over her, let them linger long on her face, her lips, her breasts. And beneath the fierceness of his gaze, Leah

felt that whisper of her womanliness grow to a pulsing
driving force, threatening to break over her with fright
ening power.

'You look surprisingly well in that gown, my dear
You must have had an interesting time of it while I was
gone, McCullough.'

Leah sucked in a harsh breath at Greville's words.

Rapidly Cole swung around, and she looked past him
to see the Colonel's caped shoulders and plumed ha
filling the entrance to the chamber. The sight of him
froze her blood, quelled and killed what had been so
alive in her but a moment before. Fear shot to her
throat.

And then Cole McCullough's voice, low but sure
came back to her.

'I told you I would help you and I meant it.'

Hands on his hips, black boots beating a rapid staccato
on the rock floor, Colonel Greville advanced into the
room.

'Corporal Bullard!' Greville's voice held drill field
peremptoriness, summoning from the darkness beyond
the thick-set man who had attacked Leah. 'Bring out the
finest bottle of Port from the cache and three glasses. I
feel a toast is in order!'

Grudgingly, Bullard slouched forward to obey orders
the heavy belly beneath the whiskey-stained tunic moving as he moved. He skirted Leah, his beady eyes
shifting over her figure, and with sly intent he touched
the brim of his dirty forage cap to her. Instinctively
Leah moved a step closer to Cole McCullough's broad
back.

'The Cherokee Rose!'

Greville dropped to one knee. Reverently he lifted

the rose cockade from the ground, and as he stared at it,
the colourless eyes danced with black lights.

'You must have dropped it, McCullough—even as I
dropped it on the raid. And how fortunate for you that I
did, eh? As you said, it was the clue that led you here.'
One hand closed hard about the white petals. 'Back
where you belong! But I shall keep it now. For luck! For
victory in the coming battle. Yes . . . the coming battle.'

Greville's voice was very quiet, but there was something in it that drove a tremor of foreboding up Leah's
spine.

The Colonel came to his feet, gauntleted hands
clasped behind him. 'Perhaps it would interest you to
know, McCullough,' he continued in a strangely ebul-
lient tone, 'that the caravan Screaming Eagle plucked
this fair flower from is made up entirely of enemies of the
Confederacy!' He turned slowly to Leah, a sinister glee
on the finely chiselled face. 'Oh, yes, my dear, I know all
about your wagon train of Yankee sodbusters! Screaming Eagle's scouts have been watching you since the day
you left Fort Laramie. Good man, Screaming Eagle, for
an ignorant savage. It's been most helpful that he speaks
a smattering of English, most helpful indeed.'

Abruptly, Greville began a fervent pacing, and in his
restless steps, in the thin body, there was the nerved-up
readiness of a blooded stallion, eager for the hunt, ready
for the kill.

Leah's foreboding deepened.

'Yes, the Indians have proved most helpful! And it
took so little to win them over! Guns, ammunition, and
the promise that if they aid us, we'll see to it that their
lands are restored.' A smile stretched over the twisted
lips that was no smile at all. 'Of course, once the

Yankees are defeated, the only land those red devils will ever see are the cotton fields of my plantation—where they'll work beside the rest of my slaves!'

Greville pulled up short before the table. 'But enough of this talk! It's time for a toast.'

With half-hypnotic dread, Leah watched Greville fill the three glasses Bullard had set out, watched him proffer one to Cole. In a trembling grasp she took her own. The swell of suspicion had risen and risen within her until now it needed only Greville's final words to turn it into a terrifying certainty.

In one slender, well-shaped hand Colonel Pierce Greville raised his goblet high.

'We drink to the annihilation of all the enemies of the South—and to the success of this morning's campaign in particular.' His voice lifted to exultation. 'We drink to the complete destruction of the wagon train!'

CHAPTER
SIX

THE goblet slipped from Leah's nerveless fingers, the sound of splintering glass echoing through the empty chamber. With stricken eyes she watched the red wine spill across the rock floor, slowly, thickly . . . like blood.

Like the blood that had seeped across those still bodies at Fort Laramie.

And at that thought, rage stabbed at Leah like the cut of a knife. A rage that brought to the fore the faces of Birdie Gordon and Alonzo Simms and Sourdough O'Rourke. A rage that overwhelmed fear and shock and even sensibility, and sent her forward against Colonel Pierce Greville wielding her anger like a rapier.

'How dare you! How dare you take innocent lives! The men and women on that wagon train mean you no harm! You have no right—'

Her surging words halted in a cry of disbelief as Cole struck her across the face.

Leah dropped into a chair, cupped hand pressed to her cheek. Stunned and defeated she stared up at Cole, her eyes dark with hurt, her lips parted. The blow had been a light one, but by its very suddenness it had vanquished her, slicing her fine ire in two.

'Take that as a warning, my girl,' Cole said softly, and his words struck an alarm through Leah's brain.

A warning indeed. He had told her he would help her but it was Pierce Greville's game they must play.

'I like my women docile and quiet,' Cole continued meaningfully. 'Do you understand?'

Leah nodded once, lifting a soft yet steady voice 'Yes—yes, I understand.'

A flare of answering surety lit Cole's eyes, and for just that moment Leah allowed herself the luxury of warming herself in his gaze. For just that moment the fear fled from her face, the horror from her heart.

For just that moment—even as on that first night—something vital and unspoken leapt between them, a promise, a hope.

Cole lifted his goblet, his eyes holding hers over the rim, and Leah knew the gesture as a wordless seal to their bond. A glow of grim determination fired her brain, braced her body, its cool flame honed on the steel that was Cole McCullough.

Cole swung a lazy shoulder to the wall. 'The girl has learned her lesson,' he offered easily. 'We won't be bothered by her again.'

'We had better not be! I'm growing weary of her sharp tongue.'

Greville's words fell cold and harsh and he drew a long breath, seemingly seeking control. The restless pacing began again, the light tapping of his fingertips on the coiled black lash a drum beat against which his nervous steps marched.

Leah's hands clenched on either side of the chair as she battled back a consuming dread. But though her body was still, her eyes followed those fitful steps, and that strange feather-light sound of hand against lash echoed in her ears. Again and again, over and over,

came that tapping, like the insistent beating of a bird's
wings against the bars of its cage.

Again and again, over and over, like the insistent
beating of Pierce Greville's madness against the bars of
his mind.

The Colonel stopped suddenly and dropped into a
chair. Consideringly he passed his goblet beneath the
high-bridged nose, the thin nostrils flaring appreciat-
ively. He took a single slow sip.

'Perhaps you'd care to hear the strategy I have plan-
ned for this morning, McCullough,' he went on in a voice
dreamily soft. 'I had thought to attack when the wagons
rounded Table Rock, but Screaming Eagle's slight trans-
gression has no doubt alerted the Yankees to our
presence. So—I've been forced to hurry my hand.
At dawn's first light the Indians will ride on the
train, thereby creating the necessary diversion for my
men.'

Greville sprang up. With a determined gesture he
replaced his goblet on the table. 'All rather like the First
Manassas Campaign, eh, McCullough?' He slapped
together the gauntleted hands. 'Just think, soon—soon
you'll be going again into battle!'

Cole downed his drink. From under half lowered lids,
the tawny eyes regarded Greville lazily for a moment.

But Leah knew that seeming idleness was but illusion.
For within that careless body was the springing strength
of a panther. Down to the supple fingers that curled
around the stem of his goblet, he stood poised and
ready.

With negligent grace, Cole pushed off the wall. He set
down his glass. 'I want no part of your campaign,
Greville.'

Pierce Greville's eyes bulged from their sockets, his brows lifting into angry crescents. He took a step forward, and across a chamber filled with smothering silence, the two men faced each other.

'Captain McCullough!' Greville's voice bit like acid. 'I'm ordering you to ride with us!'

Cole shook his head.

'I told you when I came, I ride alone these days.'

Corporal Bullard barrelled violently forward, black brows crowding across his bulging forehead. 'What kind of fools do you take us for, McCullough? You just heard all our plans, you know the location of this cave! You'll ride with us or you'll never walk out of here alive!'

With a suddenness that took Leah's breath, Cole's right hand whipped down and he drew his revolver. A corner of his mouth shot up in a sardonic half-smile. 'I'm walking out of here right now, Bullard.'

Without turning his head, without taking his eyes from the two men, Cole extended his free hand to Leah, and though her throat was thick with fear, she slipped a steady hand into his. He drew her carefully behind him. 'I'm taking the girl and I'm leaving.'

'Are you?' Greville asked softly, his colourless eyes dilating and darkening until they were blazing coals in the ivory mask of his face.

Quick as death itself, he sent the black lash sizzling through the air to cut the revolver from Cole's hands.

Swiftly, Cole lunged for his gun—and this time the whip sang out at Leah. A strangled cry caught in her throat as the black coil hovered over her white skin, then fell deliberately across the hem of her dress, slashing it to tatters.

A sneer touched Greville's twisted lips. 'I once used

this whip to keep my slaves in order. It's rather effective, don't you think?' He looked at Leah. 'I wonder how the girl would look with red stripes marking those ivory shoulders.'

Cole fell back a step. 'Don't harm her,' he said tersely. 'Do what you will with me, but let the girl go.'

Greville laughed, a high note of hysteria in that laughter that pealed through the chamber and rang out faint and ghostly in the regions beyond like a demon chorus. The hair on Leah's neck tingled. Madness. It was in the chamber with them now, suddenly freed from its bonds and swirling through the air like a phantom gust of wind.

Greville played the whip along the floor, flicking it back and forth, and his eyes gleamed fever-bright. 'You've been insubordinate, Captain McCullough! If you want the girl—' he pulled the lash meaningfully through his fingers, 'you'll have to take her.'

Grasping Greville's intent, Leah cried out a swift, piteous protest.

'No! Cole, you mustn't—'

Heavy hands spun her suddenly into a hard grip, the well-remembered, sour scent of whiskey and unwashed flesh assailing her nostrils. Close above her she saw the disgusting relish in Corporal Bullard's beady eyes.

Near gagging, Leah went rigid with loathing. Frantically she tried to arc her body away from Bullard's brutal grasp, but he twined a thick arm about her waist and caught her fast. Viciously he jerked her head up and back.

'This is one show you'll want to see, my girl,' he taunted her. He tangled sausage-fat fingers in her hair, then lifted a lock to rub it against his greasy cheek. 'And when the show is done—' his voice trailed off meaningfully.

Cole rounded on Bullard, reaching automatically for his gun. But his hand came up empty. With a low sound of rage, he clenched impotent fists at his sides.

Like the toll of a bell, like a death knell, Greville's voice fell clear and insidious. 'Remember what I said, McCullough. If you want the girl—you must take her.'

Cole's lips tightened. He took a step forward—and the lash sliced through the air and curled about his arm.

Sick with horror, Leah watched Greville pull away the coil to reveal a line of blood beneath the rent in the buckskin shirt. She choked on a sob, pressing the back of her hand to her white lips.

Again Cole stepped forward.

And as again the lash arched upward, Leah cried out in tortured agony. And as again the lash struck Cole's flesh, she felt the pain in her own heart.

'Please, please, Cole,' she pleaded with him through trembling lips, her voice thick with tears, 'please, come no farther—'

But once more he came apace. Once more the whip bit downward.

With malicious pleasure Greville struck at his shoulders, and then a second time and a third. Cole winced involuntarily at the pain, turning his head and gritting his teeth, and Leah flung herself against Bullard's grip, stretching out her arms to Cole, sobbing his name. Savagely, Bullard yanked her back. In utter despair she dropped her head and covered her face with shaking hands.

And then a tentative ray of hope sparked within her.

For through her interlaced fingers, she saw Cole's revolver lying directly before her.

Slowly, carefully, Leah tilted up her head, casting a bare, half glance at Bullard. His jaw was slack, mouth hanging open, eyes glazed with brutish anticipation as he watched Greville snake the lash along the floor.

'I promise you, McCullough,' the Colonel whispered, one corner of the twisted lips twitching violently, 'the next time I shall cut you to ribbons.'

Body drawn so tight with tension she was sure her quivering nerves would snap and sound a warning, Leah waited until Cole took another step, waited until Greville brandished the whip. As Bullard's eager eyes followed the evil upward arc of the lash, she plunged madly against his arms and grasped the revolver.

'Cole!' she cried, tossing the gun to him.

With an oath, Bullard reached for his own holster, and this time it was Leah who clutched at him, trying frantically to restrain him. He struck her down brutally and grabbed for his gun, but before the bloated fingers touched metal, Cole fired.

Red flame spouted from Cole's revolver, the chamber rocking with the explosion, the echoes bouncing like thunder between the rock walls. Bullard swayed drunkenly, pawing the air in frantic pain, and then he stiffened and fell forward.

Leah's warning scream came simultaneously with Greville's leap, as twisting like a snake, he seized Cole's discarded knife. Slashing, stabbing, face contorted into something no longer human, Greville hurled himself at Cole with a killing rage. The two men pitched backwards.

For a moment that might have been forever, they

grappled in silent fury, their death struggle magnified in the leaping shadows that flared on the wall above them, the silver blade of the knife flashing between them. Leah's hands knotted together and her lips began moving in a wordless prayer.

The writhing shadows ceased. Cole came to his knees, chest and shoulders heaving, and withdrew the bloodied knife from Greville's body. Slowly he sheathed it.

Leah felt the weakness of relief in every bone and muscle, and deep within her was the need to run to Cole, hold him close, offer him solace. But he rose swiftly, standing strong and firm once more. So soon was he in command again, so soon was he Cole McCullough again. He did not need her, now or ever, and she could only press into the shadows, letting the darkness hide the tenderness on her face.

'The marks of the lash,' she said in a voice of quiet carefulness, 'they need attention.'

Cole shook his head. 'We haven't time.' Deliberately he stepped over Greville's body, and as he did so, the movement jarred open lifeless fingers to show the rose cockade.

Cole's face set, so brittle it seemed a word might shatter it, his body drawn tight as a bow. But within the amber eyes was the same look Leah had seen the night of the fire, as if he were looking far away, years away, a world away. As if he were saying farewell.

'I'm sorry,' she said softly—and quickly he turned to look at her.

In that instant understanding flashed between them. For her sorrow was not for the death of the two men that lay there, but for the death of the past. His past—and hers, and that of a country. A past before Gettysburg, before Appomattox, before bitterness.

Cole bent and lifted his revolver and holstered it. 'We've got to get out of here,' he said tersely. 'There's no telling when the others will discover what's happened, and when they do, we'd better be well on our way.'

Leah blinked. *Was* there a way out of this nightmare? 'But how—'

Cole seized her wrist, propelling her into the shadows as he spoke. 'I overheard some of the men talking, about a second way out of this cave. The passage opens from this room. They use it as an escape route—keep the horses picketed near the entrance.'

He lifted the lantern and swung it high, squinting into its yellowed light as the beam fell first over the treasure cache, and then beyond, to a tiny crevice no wider than the breadth of a man's body.

Cole nodded in satisfaction. 'That's it.' He looked swiftly back to Leah. 'Come.'

Leah stared at his dark face, stared past him, to the unyielding blackness, and the terrified thudding of her heart seemed to shake through her entire body. But to delay even an instant might cost the lives of every man, woman, and child on the wagon train.

She stumbled forward, catching the tattered hem of her dress on a protruding piece of rock as she went. She freed herself, then with sudden determination took the silken folds in both hands and ripped away the rest of the bottom length. Whatever lay ahead, she could better face it unencumbered.

Her work done, Leah let the gown slip from her hands—realising too late the flashing show of thigh and leg she'd just put on. Her head shot up, and as she met the glint in Cole's eyes, she knew that nothing had escaped him.

'That was the second tempting display you've given today, Miss Cabot.' He chuckled, the amber eyes sparkling wickedly. 'Are you becoming wanton?'

Leah's cheeks went scorching hot, but the jeering note in his voice goaded her on like the cut of spurs. Grimly, she followed him through the forbidding slice of earth ahead.

With one hand Cole held the lantern, with the other he traced a careful way along the walls. Like a cat he prowled the sinuous twistings of the passage, the pale flare of the lantern showing the lean line of his jaw and cheek. In his shadow, Leah moved tautly, moved through an emptiness so profound, a silence so deep, she could hear her very breathing. Stalactites hung above them like shining icicles, the walls a fresco of swirling stone.

Cole stopped short. 'It dips down just ahead,' he warned.

They dropped to their hands and knees, crawling through the narrow tunnel. Leah's breath came fast with exertion, again and again the rough outcroppings of rock tore at her flesh. She tightened her mouth against the pain, brushed the hair from her face.

And always before her, alert and untiring, was Cole McCullough.

The ceiling lifted and Cole came to one knee, flinging out a restraining arm. Drawing herself to a sitting position, Leah strained her eyes past him to see the darkness ahead fall sharply away. Far below them stretched a vast and seemingly bottomless cavern, the only way across a shelf that jutted out a bare foot from the wall.

Cole stood.

'Follow me,' he said briefly, 'and don't look down.'
He glanced back over his shoulder and questioning eyes
plumbed the depths of Leah's strength. She managed a
nod in return, a small smile.

With steps that never faltered, Cole moved onto the
ledge and across the precipice.

Hands splayed to either side of her, her back scraping
flat against the rock wall, Leah followed the steady
thread of his path. She was nearly to safety when it
happened.

A loose piece of stone gave way beneath her. For one
terrifying instant her foot slipped over the edge. Her
heart lurched and she drew back. A cold sweat broke out
over her body. Dumbly she looked at the waiting abyss
below. It seemed to rise up, reach out for her—

'Leah!'

Cole's voice cracked like a pistol shot.

'Look at me,' he called to her, and then again, his
words a ringing command. 'Look at me!'

Slowly, slowly Leah turned her head. Like a lifeline,
Cole's gaze met hers. She edged a tentative step forward. Then another—and another—and then strong
hands were around her waist, sweeping her to safety.

'We must—we must go on—' Her breath came in
great shuddering gasps, burning through her lungs, as
she fought against weariness, fought against fear, struggled to stay erect. Struggled to hold out a little longer.
'We must hurry! We've got to get to the wagon train in
time—'

'Get to the wagon train in time,' Cole repeated blankly. His narrowed eyes scanned her face. 'What the devil
are you talking about?'

Leah's voice came in a stammering frenzy, her words a rush of hope. 'Then—you don't think there will be a raid—You think that with Greville dead—his men—'

'I think his death won't mean a damn to that rabble,' Cole broke in impatiently. 'When they discover his body and Bullard's, they'll simply elect a new leader. Greed has no respect for death—any man's. Oh, they'll attack all right, and the Indians with them—those poor fools think they're fighting for their land! But when they do, we'll be on our way to Fort Laramie.'

'Fort Laramie!' Leah's startled gaze went wide. Slowly she shook her head, standing back against his grip. 'No, no, we can't go to Fort Laramie! The wagon train,' she murmured, 'we must return to the wagon train—'

Cole stared at her as if she'd gone mad.

'We can't go back there! Don't you understand?' His fingers bit with hard urgency, his voice falling low and swift. 'Greville's men, the Indians, they'd be right behind us. They'd sight us and cut us down in no time.'

'It's you who doesn't understand!' Leah whispered fiercely. 'We must go back, we must warn the others!'

He shook her once with rough impatience. 'Your death on a dusty road will help no one!'

Leah twisted away from him and backed against the wall, staring at him with furious eyes.

'I will go back!' she cried. 'I will! I will!' Her voice trembled and broke, tears of near hysteria starting down her cheeks. She began to give way beneath the strain of the long night of horror, her nerves shredded raw. 'I will go back! I will! And if you won't take me—I—I'll go myself!'

She spun around and into the darkness, stumbling, sobbing. Brisk footsteps sounded behind her and she quickened her pace, but Cole caught her sharply back.

'Leave me be! Let me pass! I will go back! I will! I will!'

She began to beat clenched fists against his chest, trying to break the iron cut of his grip. She kicked, she clawed, she bit, she screamed wildly at him, and through it all, through her frenzy and her tears and her tumult, Cole held her fast. Silently he took her abuse, his face as unreadable as stone.

Then suddenly she was still.

Her wild anger had been spent. All the pent-up tension and fear had been drained from her, and with it had gone the last vestiges of her remaining strength. She crumpled against Cole.

Beneath the rents in the buckskin shirt she could feel the thick mat of black hair that began at the base of his brown throat and covered his chest, feel it stinging her naked flesh. She pressed a hand to that chest, thinking how strong it was, how resolute the man.

But at her touch there was an instant tautening of his body, his hands held her away. And it was as if all comfort, all security had been taken from her.

'Please, Cole,' she whispered, 'please, please hold me.'

A moment longer he remained rigid, and then he slid his hands up her bare arms and she felt a shudder pass through him. But no—no, surely the trembling was of her own body, wedded now so close to his she could feel every potent line of him.

His hard muscled thighs were pressed against her, his heavy chest crushing her breasts. His arms were tight about her waist, her shoulders, and Leah knew that within the circle of those arms nothing in this world, nor the next, could harm her.

He bent his head, burying his face in her hair, then he wound one hand through the tumbled thickness and with a jerk so savage her eyes watered with the pain, he yanked up her head.

His forehead was wet with sweat, as if from some great effort, the muscles of his face working tensely. The arm around Leah's waist hardened to steel, all gentleness gone from his touch, and against that frightening power, Leah felt her own strength as no more than a reed in the wind.

'You're hurting me,' she whispered, and at her plea, his lips thinned to a cruel line beneath the dark moustache.

'Am I?' he questioned with a cool brutality.

Quickly Cole caught her arms and twisted them behind her, bending her backwards before him. His teeth clenched hard, his jaw muscles trembling, and she could feel the fury pulsing through him, feel the heat of his rage, see the demons that danced in his eyes. Demons from that private hell that remained a secret still.

Steadily Leah met those haunted eyes.

The tear stains were fresh on her cheeks, Bullard's bruise beginning to swell and darken against her forehead, yet from that white and exhausted face, her gaze shone forth serenely. And as if she would gentle him with her eyes, she let that gaze roam his face, probe the dark depths of it.

'Don't look at me like that!'

The anger of his arms increased, a raw note of violence shot through his words. 'I tell you—don't look at me like that!'

But there was that in Leah that could not be stilled, that rushed out to meet his rage. A dignity that could not be shattered, a gentleness that, fight against it though he might, he could not break.

And before her gaze, his own eyes dropped away. His grip slackened and he swung around on his heel, forearming the sweat from his face. Abruptly his voice came from the shadows.

'I'll take you back to the wagon train.'

Leah's lips parted with sudden gratefulness, but she did not speak. She knew he would accept nothing from her, not even simple thanks.

He accepted nothing, he asked nothing. He gave nothing.

Cole lifted the lantern, and as the yellow sheen of light fell full over the steep rock wall ahead, Leah could not contain her cry of gladness. For balanced against that wall was a crude wooden ladder.

Swiftly Cole mounted the rungs. After an ascertaining glance without, he beckoned to Leah and she emerged from the black hole to find a world leaden with the grey of predawn. The cave opened into the crest of a hill, and dropping flat, Leah beside him, Cole carefully parted the thicket of brush that crowned the summit for a view of the scene below.

At the foot of the slope was a rope corral, the dim silhouettes of Indian ponies and saddle horses moving within, and some distance beyond, Greville's men were gathered about a campfire. They lolled idly on the ground, some propped up on one elbow, a bottle or two passing between them. Sentries had been posted at the edge of the camp, but they, too, stood carelessly, drinking, chewing on tobacco, their rifles hanging slack.

Yet even as the white men took their ease, the Indians were working themselves into a frenzy.

Sitting cross-legged by the fire, several of the braves were beating on drums of tightly-strung skins, while others moved in concentric circles around the flames, leaping and screeching, patting their lips as they cried out to produce eerie tremolos of sound, shaking rattles to underscore their footbeats. Their leggings were brave with beads, their feathered headdresses hanging to their shoulders and below, their faces and torsos streaked red with paint. The flat, steady rhythm of their drums filled the world, and the skies rang with the shrill sounds of their whoops and shrieks. Against the haze of wood smoke, their capering, fitful figures rose up ghostly and half-real.

'Why are they dancing?' Leah questioned softly.

'It's part of their war ritual, they're making good medicine for the battle.' Cole smiled grimly. 'And they're providing us with excellent cover.' He came to a crouch. 'I'm going for the horse.'

Without thought Leah reached out a hand to him, palm up, as if she would offer sustenance—strength. But he did not see the gesture. Or seeing, did not care. Without even a glance at her, Cole pushed out from behind the crest of the slope. Leah's hand fell to the ground. Helplessly, her eyes followed his dark figure down the hill.

Body hunched low, a hand at the ready on his revolver, Cole traced a swift, soundless course from one clump of brush or mound of rocks to another, pausing only seconds behind each sheltering screen of sage and stone before he pressed on to the next. As he neared the corral, the horses lifted their heads, their ears going back, and the black gelding gave a snort of recognition. Quickly Cole ran a silencing hand over the animal's flank. He untied the horse, then keeping well within the shelter of the jagged shadows, led him back up the hill.

Once he'd gained the rise, Cole vaulted into the saddle. He extended a hand to Leah and with one powerful pull, swung her up behind him. 'Hold hard,' he commanded tersely, 'it's going to be a rough ride.'

Obediently Leah wound her arms around his back, the sudden, strong nearness of him bringing the colour to her cheeks, the heat to her body. She was tinder, raked to flame at his touch.

Cole turned his mount, touching rowled spurs to its flanks. In sudden fury the horse leapt forward.

As the wind they went.

Wildly they plunged down the slope of one hill, then up another, the earth rising up to meet them, then falling away. The gelding was stretched long and low, his hooves spouting dust. They crashed into a patch of brush and broke through, and the trail entered a gorge. Right they slanted, left, the horse twisting in mid-air, his nostrils distended, black coat flecked with foam.

Cole was taut in the saddle, urging the horse on, on, Leah's hair streaming behind like a pennon. There was fear in her heart, and urgency, but there was exhilaration, too.

The cool, clear wind cut at her face, her senses quickening to the stride of the racing horse, to the spinning earth. To Cole McCullough.

She was heady with the leaping rhythm of his body beneath her hands, filled with hot, secret joy. She leaned her cheek against his hard muscled back and his name was a wordless whisper within her.

These pounding moments, carved from the separateness of their lives, might be all she would ever have of him. But she would not think of that now. Now it was enough to feel her being melding, dissolving into his, feel their bodies beating together as if with a single pulse.

This time before dawn, this ebb time, was theirs alone. It could never be taken from her.

They topped the crest of the Table Rock to see the circled caravan waiting below, its white canvas hoods touched an ominous crimson by the first flush of morning. Cole spurred the gelding to a final burst of speed. Headlong they surged down the slope towards the settler's camp.

At the frantic hoofbeats, the guards sprang to position, rifles levelled. Newly awakened men, women, and children spilled from their wagons. Within the protective circle Cole drew rein, checking the horse so swiftly he drew back on his haunches. At once a small crowd converged on them, Birdie Gordon battling past the others for the first words.

'Child, I never been so happy to see another human bein' in all my born days! We've been a'searchin' for you the whole dang night—' The woman stopped, face twisting into awful awareness as her blunt blue eyes ran the length of Leah's tattered white gown. Birdie's voice fell to appalled wonder. 'What have you been through child? What's been done to you?'

'Hush your chatter, woman!'

The fiddler elbowed Birdie out of the way, and reaching up skinny arms, lifted Leah from the saddle.

'Can't you see this gal is tuckered out?'

As her feet touched solid ground, Leah's knees went weak. Her legs were cramped and stiff, her body aching in previously unknown places. For the first time she was conscious of the welts on arms and face where she'd been slashed by brush.

'I—I was taken by the renegades,' she managed in a dry whisper. Her words brought a wave of sound and Leah strained to speak above it. 'Taken to their camp.' She gestured to the silent man still astride the black horse. 'He—he saved my life—'

'Did he now?'

Eb Hutter stalked forward. He wore a union suit and trousers, suspenders hanging, and his flat face was creased with sleep, his eyes bloodshot. Behind him, his pallid wife stood with two small girls clutching at her knees, a coarse blanket about her nightgown.

'And ain't this a pretty how-do-ye-do?' Hutter went on, animosity stirring his thin shoulders. 'Mr Cole McCullough hightails it outta Fort Laramie jest after the renegades attack, then the next thing we know, he turns up at their camp. Kinda makes a man wonder what Mr Cole McCullough's been up to.'

Cole swung down from the saddle. 'I see nothing's changed, Hutter.' With swift, violent movements he yanked his saddlebags free and slung them over a shoulder, then jerked his rifle from its sheath. He turned. 'You're still the curious type.'

The sodbuster's mouth worked convulsively. 'If you mean do I still got questions, I do, and I aim to get the answers!'

Frantically Leah thrust herself between the two men. 'We haven't time for questions now!' Catching sight of the wagonmaster bearing down on them at a brisk trot, she spun on her heel. 'Mr Simms!'

Leah plunged towards him, skidding against his burly frame. 'Mr Simms, we've just come from the renegade camp, come to warn you! The renegades—the Indians—they're on their way here! They're going to attack the train!'

Renegades! Indians! Attack!

Pandemonium broke loose. Here and there the settlers rushed, like a swarm of ants around their nest, their feet moving to a desperate rhythm.

The wagonmaster seized Leah by the shoulders, staring into her strained face. 'You sure of what you jest said, little lady?'

'Yes! Oh, yes!' His convulsive grip made her gasp with pain. 'We must hurry!'

Simms broke from her, his boots sending the gravel flying, and hoisted himself atop a wagon seat.

'Settle down, every one of ya! Settle down!'

Simms' bellow stopped the settlers in their tracks, besting their churning frenzy. Whitely they stared up at him. In a voice that rang like a bugle, the wagonmaster rolled out the drumfire of his orders.

'Tote down every barrel and chest in the wagons and heft 'em clear to the canvas! Gather up your weapons and your shot, water and bandages. Don't fire until I give the signal, and when you do fire, pick your target and aim careful! If we keep our heads and don't waste our powder, we'll do all right!'

Unbound hair streaming over their shoulders, feet flying, the women gathered up children and guns. Tight-lipped, grim-faced, the men piled the barricades high. Shoulder to shoulder they worked, struggling to subdue their thudding hearts, united in faith—and fear.

Only two men stood rooted. Two men locked in their own moment, the frenetic world around them no more than a backdrop for their anger.

Caught in the crossfire of their hatred, powerless to move, Leah looked from one to the other. Looked from the simmering, boiling core of Eb Hutter to the fire and ice that was Cole McCullough. The amber eyes were agate hard, yet with a carefully controlled ferocity that sparked like flame.

'This ain't finished between us,' Hutter bit off savagely. 'Not by a long shot.'

'Eb!' Abigail Hutter's wail pierced the current of tension. 'Eb! Please! We need you!'

Grudgingly the sodbuster backed up his loose-limbed body, but his gaze stayed stiffened on Cole. 'I meant what I said—I aim to get them answers.'

'Save your strength, Hutter.' Cole's mouth quirked to a contemptuous line. 'You're going to need it.'

And as if in eerie echo of his words, an explosion of blood-chilling shrieks rent the air. In a single line, bodies glistening copper in the new minted sun, the Indians swarmed down the hill.

The attack had begun.

CHAPTER
SEVEN

WITHOUT ceremony, Cole thrust Leah to her knees, dropping to a crouch beside her. 'Can you reload?'

'I can learn.'

She'd said that once before. Then she'd doubted her own words. But now— It was a world away from then, and she was a different girl.

Cole dropped his saddle bags into her lap. 'Keep the shot coming,' he tossed over his shoulder, crawling for the barricades, 'and keep low.'

Hoofbeats roared like dull thunder, the Indians racing ever nearer, nearer. Bows and quivers of arrows were slung across their backs, war hatchets at their belts. They held carbines aloft, waving them over their heads as their voices rose full-throated and hideous in a cacophony of shrieks and yelps.

Lying prone behind the piled boxes and barrels, the settlers watched them come. Watched and waited, men and boys with rifles to their shoulders, their womenfolk clutching ammunition belts or powderhorns and bullet pouches. Silent they were, still, their eyes stark and unflinching on the horizon. Here and there a man swallowed against his fear, Adam's apple bobbing in his dry throat, here and there a woman doubled her hands into fists.

Leah could feel her own fear like cold fingers, creeping across her body. She could not move, nor breathe, nor blink. Could only watch the bobbing fringe of Indians come on and on. Faster, harder, louder, they pounded, until the earth vibrated with the sound of their horses' hooves, until one could see the dark coals of their eyes in their lean, red faces. Until the seconds stretched to eternity.

Yet still the wagonmaster did not give the signal to fire.

Abruptly, as if sliced by a knife, the line of warriors split in two. Veering left and right, they encircled the wagons. Alonzo Simms came to his knees.

'Now!'

The air shook as fifty rifles fired at once.

Dropping to the far side of their mounts, hanging on by a leg, the Indians fired from beneath their horse's necks, the fusillade of their shots merging with the medley of their whoops and howls. They circled again, closer this time. The white men unleashed a second volley, a third, firing at will. Within the circled wagons, the tethered oxen and horses began a terrified stamping at the cracking of the guns.

Her rifle propped against a wagon spoke, Birdie was firing steadily into the mêlée. Beside her, running a ramrod down his ancient flintlock, Sourdough. A shot whizzed over his head, just out of range of his top hat. Cussing vigorously, Birdie took aim at the Indian who had fired. As he toppled from his horse, she whooped in delight. 'Take that, you mangy varmint!'

'Can't stand me a sassy female,' Sourdough grumbled, hefting his musket. The venerable old weapon bucked and roared, nearly knocking the fiddler flat. Non-

chalantly he righted his hat, shifted his cigar, and fired
again.

Cole had come to one knee. Steadily he aimed into the
assault, coolly. He dropped an Indian backwards over
his running pony, another he sent sprawling to the
ground. Emptying his rifle, he flung it to the ground and
drew his Colt, and hastily Leah grabbed up the discarded
weapon. She'd watched Birdie reload, and now she
forced her own clumsy fingers through the motions,
seizing fresh cartridges, then slamming them into the
chamber. Burnt powder stung her eyes as she worked,
clogged her throat. Ever higher, ever thicker, the dust
swirled around her, around them all.

Leah lifted her head, exchanging rifle for revolver,
and through the hazy veiling of black smoke and brown
dust, she saw again the Table Rock, crowned with
riders.

These men rode in no fine, shining line, they displayed
no skilled horsemanship. Liquored up, leaderless,
counting on the surprise attack and the Indians to turn
the day into a debacle, the renegades rode
lazily—contemptuously—into battle.

But forewarned, forearmed, the settlers were fighting
doughtily. Secure behind their solid, if hastily erected
defences, they offered the smallest possible target, yet
they were able to aim with far greater accu-
racy than mounted men astride galloping horses. They
poured fire at the flashing riders, round after round,
until the world was a bedlam of screaming shot.

One of the defenders slumped backwards from the
barricades, a hand clutched to his shoulder, blood seeping from between his splayed fingers. Hastily Leah bent
over him, lifting a canteen to his lips. But as she fumbled

or bandages, he shook his head, motioning her away.

'I kin manage. Ain't no time to bother 'bout a flesh wound.'

Grimly, gritting his teeth against the pain, the man resumed firing.

Cole threw down his revolver and reached for his rifle, levelling it against his shoulder. Once again the flare of his gunfire rolled remorselessly on, demonically accurate. With every shot he downed an enemy, working his weapon with a ruthlessness that sent the perspiration streaming unchecked down his forehead. Catching up a strip of bandaging, Leah leaned forward to wipe the sweat from his eyes, his face. But at the touch of her hand on his arm, he turned and gave her a single look.

A look without fear, without life, the look of a man who has seen too much for too long. 'And how do you like the sounds and sights of war, Miss Cabot? Not much like your drawing-room teas, is it?'

His words hit with the bitter force of a blow, and at those words, at the look in his eyes, Leah dropped her hands, shrinking back. Cole turned away, the sound of his gunfire drowning out his savage laughter.

With the swiftness of desperation, the renegades began retreating, fleeing over the crest of the hill. Yet the Indians did not follow. Fired by the fanaticism of those who fight not for greed, but for an idea, they massed for a second attack. Having emptied their firearms, they drew their bows, lifted their tomahawks. Voices blending into a single hellish howl, they bore down on the train.

The settlers did not flinch. Behind their barricades, the wounded and dying littered the ground—but there was no weeping. Not now. Rather, women took up their

fallen husband's rifles, children wrested weapons from
their parents' lifeless hands. Like the Sioux and Cheyenne, they were fighting for an idea—for their right to
this land.

In a whirling, reckless circle of plunging horses and
flying manes, of upflung arms and flashing arrows, the
Indians circled the train. They heeled their ponies close,
leaping over the barricades. Point-blank, the settlers
fired at the red, screeching forms.

A hideously-painted face topped a wagon. A copper
body arose. The Indian levelled a lance, hurling himself
at Cole. With no time to fire, Cole swung his rifle like
club, crashing the heavy barrel against the warrior's
skull. The brave toppled backwards. But even as he fell
a second Indian swung into the breach.

Leah seized the freshly loaded revolver, her bullet
stopping the Indian mid-stride. The tomahawk trembled
in the red hand, the furious eyes went vacant. The brave
fell to the earth beside her.

Leah stared at the still body. A round hole, circled
black gaped in the centre of his chest, blood gushing
from it, spattering her dress. Leah transferred her gaze
to the weapon in her hands.

She had no remembrance of firing it. But she had. She
had. She had done what she must.

'I'll be dad-gummed!' Sourdough's voice rang out
jubilantly. 'We got 'em on the run!'

Half-dazed, Leah looked up, following the line of the
fiddler's arm to the horizon. It was true. The Indians
were riding towards the Table Rock. As swiftly as it had
begun, it had ended.

And now there was only the stinging smell of burnt
gunpowder and scorched flesh, the gasps of the wounded

ed, the soft keening of the bereaved. And on both sides of the barricades, the stillness of death.

Cole lifted his gun from Leah's grasp. 'My compliments, Miss Cabot. Your aim is improving. A little more practice and you'll be an expert shot.'

Leah stared at him. In the face of the circled destruction within the wagons and without, his words held a cruel callousness. Softly she asked, 'Does human life mean so little to you?'

For a second Cole's face twisted violently, his lips twitching. Then he stiffened. Head averted, he answered her carefully. 'When you've lived with death long enough, nothing, not even life, means much.'

The wagonmaster came to his feet, gaze steady as he surveyed the camp.

'We'd best be settin' things aright,' Simms said. 'The sooner we start thinkin' 'bout what's ahead and fergit what's happened here, the better it'll be.'

Solid words, fraught with simple wisdom, and the hope of days to come. On the strength of those words the survivors arose, one by one, slowly, collecting themselves to face what lay ahead.

Simms pivoted, turning to move among them, and as he did so, a swift shadow slithered up from the side of a wagon. Too late Leah saw the gleaming, coppery face of Screaming Eagle above his drawn bow. Too late—too late—the warning cry caught in her throat.

'Die, White Chief!'

Cole leapt to his feet and fired, but even as the Indian dropped to the ground, his arrow ripped into the wagonmaster's body. The big man fell where he stood.

On hands and knees Leah covered the short distance to Alonzo Simms' prostrate form. His eyes were shut tight, teeth clenched, the feathered shaft of the arrow protruding from his heaving chest.

'Pull it out—' the words were thick with pain. 'Some-one—pull the dang thing out—'

Swiftly Cole McCullough fell to his knees beside the wagonmaster. Lips set, he seized the arrow in both hands and without a pause, jerked it free. He drew back. Breaking the arrow across his knee, he tossed it aside.

Above the collective silence of every settler's indrawn breath, Birdie Gordon barked orders.

'A couple of you galoots tote 'im to his wagon. And do it gentle like! You—fiddler! Fetch me a bucket of mud.'

The bewhiskered cheeks of Sourdough O'Rourke puffed out in protest, but his words were stifled by Birdie's quick poke to his middle.

'And no backtalk, O'Rourke! I done a heap of doctor-in' in my time and there's nothin' better than a mud poultice. If there's anyone can bring that old buffalo through, it's Birdie Gordon.'

Four men bent to do Birdie's bidding, Simms' face convulsing as they hefted him high, beads of cold sweat standing out on his forehead. Yet he managed a final word for the woman stomping along at his side.

'You are the doggonedest female—'

Leah looked to Cole. 'Will he live?'

'If the arrow wasn't poisoned, he has a chance.'

With a small, despairing gesture, Leah ran her hands over the red stains on the white dress. Only inches away, where the wagonmaster had lain, the ground was matted and wet. Prairie grass stained red with blood . . . Would the image persist all the way to California?

The sound of boots striking hard against the dry earth arrested Leah's thoughts. Quickly she lifted her head, and looked into the hooded gaze of Eb Hutter. A small semi-circle of armed men surrounded him, their thumbs notched over the hammers of their rifles, poised to draw the weapons to full-cock. From powder-grimed faces, their eyes regarded Cole warily.

'Me and the boys come to git them answers, McCullough, 'bout how you figure in with the renegades. And we mean to git them answers with no trouble from you.' The sodbuster's mouth quirked to an ugly line. 'So throw down yer shootin' iron!'

Hutter's voice was deadly, lifting Leah's memories of those moments by Grandfather John's grave. Only this time it was more than apprehension that gnawed at her insides, more almost than fear. A premonition of disaster, fed by those minutes before the attack, fuelled by the secret she alone shared with Cole, stirred within her. Still on her knees, she clenched her hands in her lap, clenched them hard.

Cole stood. Casually he unbuckled his holster and threw it to the ground. With equal languor he unsheathed his Bowie knife and tossed it down. Into the tense silence he laughed softly. 'That ought to make you rest easier, Hutter.'

The cool words sent the sodbuster's features trembling with hate, started the pale eyes burning with anger. He stalked forward.

'All right—now start talkin'!'

Cole smiled slowly. 'I'd be glad to tell you of my—association—with the renegades. It so happens their leader was my commander during the war. In fact, we all served together in the same army—' He paused. His lips curled down, the amber eyes narrowed to a strange gleam, and across the barricade of raised rifle barrels,

Leah could sense his sudden, keen anticipation. It ran through him like a current, drawing her to her feet with arms outstretched, as if she would ward off his coming words. But she knew she was powerless to stop the moment.

Steadily Cole looked down the file of watching, waiting faces. With deliberation he finished the sentence. 'The Confederate States of America.'

Eb Hutter's sallow face went ashen, a quiver shook his body. He whirled in fury, springing atop a wagon seat, and his flat voice exploded across the camp. 'McCullough's a Johnny Reb!'

All movement ceased. Every eye turned upward, every heartbeat halted.

'He's a Johnny Reb!' the sodbuster screamed again, a cord standing out in his skinny neck. 'One of them greybellies that killed my boys, that killed your husbands and brothers! And so were the rest of them white varmints that raided the Fort, that attacked the train! McCullough's one of 'em! One of the renegades! He's been at their camp ever since he hightailed it outta Fort Laramie—he led 'em right to us today!'

'No!' Leah cried. 'No! You're wrong—'

But her words were sighs in the wind, whispers against the rising torrent of anger.

'A Confederate?'

'One of the renegades?'

'Led 'em right to us?'

Man turned to man, friend to friend, husband to wife, trading snatches of words, snippets of sentences. Ignited by the memories of war, their past sorrows fanned by this new grief, they were dry prairie grass to the torch of Hutter's voice.

'And do you know what I say we do with the dirty Reb?'

Hutter leapt to the ground, arms outstretched as if to gather in the smouldering animosity. And in his eyes, Leah read what was coming.

'I say we hang him!'

'Hang him! Hang him!'

The words echoed back and forth. The low muttering became a roar. The tinder sparked to flame, and the blaze rolled across the camp.

'Hang him! Hang the Johnny Reb!'

The cry became a chant. The crowd became a mob. They surged forward, surrounding Cole. And against the tide, the man in buckskin stood nerveless, immobile, a side of his mouth slanting upward in a gibing half-smile as his hands were tied behind him.

With Cole in the centre, the mob pressed onward. Men in blood-stained bandages, women in battle-streaked nightdress, boys and girls trailing, all—all of them pressing towards the gnarled cottonwood that stood in solitary significance near the banks of the backwater.

Through the roiling anger, Leah struggled. She pushed and pounded against the crowd, beating on backs and shoulders, screaming to be heard.

'Please—please listen to me! Cole McCullough is innocent! He's innocent, I tell you!'

But her words went unheard. The fire was raging out of control, threatening to destroy everything in its path.

A knotted rope was thrown over a branch of the cottonwood, a horse positioned beneath the tree. Cole was lifted into the saddle.

His tattered shirt had been ripped off his shoulders,

showing the heavy chest streaked with dirt, corded with the marks of the lash. The slouch hat had been knocked to the ground and his brown hair fell long over his forehead. His face was shaded with a bruise.

But he had not been humbled.

Leah halted. Stock still, the mob boiling about her, she watched Cole's crooked half-smile become a grin, teeth bared white in his sun-bronzed, powder-blackened face. No, he had not been humbled. And no matter what happened, Leah knew he never would be.

Knew, too, he would never say a word in his own defence.

Challengingly, contemptuously, as if he were casting his carelessness against their violence, his gaze roved the crowd.

And then his eyes met Leah's.

For just an instant a kind of tautness came into his face, his lips tightened. His gaze passed on.

Leah felt her breath sear her throat, her lungs. Stiff as a pointer, she wheeled about, running again. She slid to her knees beside Cole's discarded holster and seized the gun. Gasping for air like a drowning person, she staggered to her feet and pushed on.

'Throw down your weapons!'

The crowd hushed. In slack-jawed amazement, the two men with rifles stared at Leah. She motioned to them with the barrel of the gun.

'You heard me—throw down your weapons!'

Hutter guffawed aloud. He held one arm upraised, the noose dangling in his hand, and with it, he gestured meaningfully to Cole.

'Don't bother us, gal, we got work to do. Besides, I don't think you got the nerve to fire that thing!'

'Think again, Mr Hutter,' Leah said clearly. 'I just shot an Indian through the heart—and I'll do the same to the next man who makes a move.'

At the tone of her voice, at the look in her eyes, Hutter's arm swung slowly downward, the men's rifles sliding from their hands to thud against the ground. Reading their thoughts, the corners of Leah's mouth stole into a bare smile. No, she thought with a touch of grim pride, this was not the well-bred Miss Cabot of Boston who stood before them!

This was a woman who had endured the torments of the trail, sent her hat flying in the face of death. This was a woman who had faced down a Pawnee Chief, endured the dark hell of the renegade's cave. This was a woman equal to her words.

Steadily Leah came forward, through the parting waves of people. And though Hutter glared at her, the consuming hatred in his eyes animal-like in its intensity, he backed off. She turned and faced the crowd.

For the space of a single breath, Leah was aware of the still air, the hot sun, fully risen now and golden. Aware, too, of the simmering and stirring of the men and women who watched her.

She knew them as good people. Good people pushed to the brink of violence by buried bitterness and fresh sadness, by too many miles and too many hardships. But she also knew that justice on the frontier was hard and vengeance swift.

They would listen—but for how long?

Leah lifted her head, her back erect.

'Cole McCullough is innocent! It's true he was in the renegade camp, but he came there only a day ago—he had nothing to do with the raid on Fort Laramie!' Leah felt Cole's gaze burning into her, boring holes through her composure, but without a break she went on. 'He didn't ride here to lead the renegades to us, he came at a risk to his own life to warn you! You saw him during the attack! Why would he have fought the way he did if he was one of them?'

'Good way to cover his tracks, I'd say,' a tall, bony homesteader countered. He stroked the grey beard that fell nearly to his waist. 'Kinda like runnin' with the hare and huntin' with the hounds.'

'You're wrong! Cole McCullough killed the renegade leader! Surely he wouldn't have done that if he was one of them! I know the truth of things, I was in the renegade camp—'

'Is that where you got the fancy dress, girl?' Hutter jeered. 'No wonder you're so willin' to take McCullough's part, spent the whole night with him in that camp, didn't ya? And I got a pretty good idea of what went on—'

'Shut your miserable face, Hutter!'

Cole threw a leg over the horse's withers and leapt to the ground. Back braced against the saddle, he kicked out at Hutter with both legs, sending him sprawling backwards.

'You'll be sorry for that, Reb!'

The sodbuster shot up. He swung a sledgehammer fist against Cole's jaw, then threw a vicious blow to his middle, doubling him over. Leah's cry and Caleb Rance's movement came at once, the miner throwing an arm around Hutter's neck and yanking him away.

'You got no right to say them things 'bout Miz Cabot, Eb!' Emma Rance called out. 'She's never been anything but a lady!' The miner's wife pushed up homespun sleeves over her hefty forearms. Towering two heads over her husband—and a head above most of the other men—she was a resolute figure. 'And if Miz Cabot says McCullough is innocent, I believe her!'

Seething, Hutter struggled against Rance's sinewy grasp. 'He's a damned greybelly!'

'Confederate though he is, have any of you realised that Cole McCullough is also the only man who can lead us to California now?'

The abrupt, ringing words levelled the anger in the crowd to sudden wariness. As if touched by some deathly enchantment, the settlers stood silent, rooted.

From the corner of her eye, Leah saw Cole slowly straighten, a trickle of blood running from one corner of his mouth, and on his face she read cold fury. Yet fiercely she cried out, 'Don't you see, Cole McCullough is the only one among us who's been West—'

Her voice cracked. Desperation pressed against her. The hot, bright sunlight glancing off the upturned faces rendered them like glass, hard and undecipherable. Wherever she looked there was only suspicion, distrust. Was there no one who would heed her—help her?

Then, newly arrived at the edge of the crowd, Birdie Gordon and Sourdough O'Rourke took up the cudgel.

'The child makes a powerful lot of sense! Our scout's dead, Mr Simms is in a mighty bad way. It appears to me that Cole McCullough is the only one who can git us through now.'

'The females is right!' the fiddler assented. 'Much as I hate to admit it.'

United in their support, the man and woman stood side by side, solid as a brick wall, and Leah threw them both a heartfelt look. She should have known she was not alone.

'I never been with a train further than Laramie,' Sourdough rumbled on, 'but I heard plenty 'bout what's ahead. We got a desert to cross and mountains to climb, and I don't fancy facin' any of it without a proper guide!'

The hooded eyes in Eb Hutter's rawboned face flashed fire. Sensing the perceptible shifting of the crowd, he tried to catch back control, spitting out his words with stinging acid. 'This here's a Northern train! Are we gonna let some Johnny Reb lead it?'

'And jest who do you reckon oughtta lead it, Hutter? You?' The fiddler gave an eloquent grunt. 'If I recollect right, it was you almost cost us our skin the night them Pawnee came callin'!'

On bandy legs Caleb Rance stumped forward. 'I don't like Johnny Rebs any better'n the rest of ya, and I fought 'em clear from Bull Run to Appomattox! But I'm itchin' to get to them gold fields, and if an ex-Confederate is the only one can git me there, I say we let him live! How do the rest of ya vote?'

For a heart-holding moment Cole McCullough's life hung poised. For a moment the balance hung between old passions and new hope. And tomorrow won.

Affirmation sparked through the crowd, overpowering Hutter's protests, and Rance turned to Cole.

'Well, McCullough?'

'I lead you to California and you let me live.' The husky voice was even, though it held a fierce, almost frightening undertone. 'Is that it?'

'That's it.'

Cole let out his breath in a small, mirthless laugh. 'Not much of a deal.'

'Mebbe not,' Rance answered levelly, 'but it's the only one you're gonna get.'

The amber eyes narrowed. 'How do you know I'll stay with the train? How do you know I won't bolt tonight, and head out on my own? After all, you don't know anything about me, where I've been, where I was headed. I misled you about being a Confederate. Maybe,' he finished slowly, 'there are other things I didn't tell you as well.'

Cole turned his head. And as his gleaming gaze searched her out, Leah sensed his stillness, as if something within were waiting.

His words had been but echoes of all the unspoken words they'd shared. This moment but a mirror of all their other moments. In the silence that stretched between them, they had come full circle.

He was daring her to tell everything, all her suspicions.

Was Cole McCullough a deserter? Or, remembering his skill with the Colt, a gunman? Or worse? Had he been escaping a posse the night he'd held a knife to her throat?

As on that first night he watched her now with yellow cat's eyes, with the half-savage eyes of a hunted animal. Watched her without fear, without entreaty. Once again he was entrapped but unafraid.

And once again she knew—as she'd known nothing else before or since that night—that she would not betray him.

'Perhaps,' Leah said softly, never glancing from him, 'we should ask Mr McCullough for his word.'

'My—word?'

A smile without humour cracked Cole's lips, one

eyebrow lifted. A strange expression flicked his features and disappeared. Abruptly he looked away from her.

'Of course you have my word,' he drawled lazily. 'My word as a—' he paused, then sent the words home with force, 'Southern gentleman.'

Rance bobbed his head, monkey face resolute. 'Guess that'll have to do.' Sheepishly he stepped behind Cole, beginning to untie the rope that bound Cole's wrists. 'Reckon we can't expect a man to lead us to California tied up.'

But bounding furiously forward, Eb Hutter threw the little miner aside. With convulsive jerks he loosened the rope, burning the cord into Cole's flesh. 'Mebbe you won this time, Reb,' he breathed in pulsing rage, 'but jest remember—I'll be watchin' ya! All the way to the banks of the Sacramento!'

The sodbuster threw down the rope and wheeled, kicking up clods of dust as he stalked away. Head averted, Cole looked after the man a moment. He brushed a hand across his bloodied mouth, then bent and lifted his hat, hitting it once against his knee to shake the dust from it.

'Bury your dead and water your stock. Don't worry about the Indians, they'll come tonight to claim their own, they always do. Let the buzzards take the renegades. You've got an hour—then we head out.'

'An hour!' Mrs Rance sputtered in disbelief. 'That don't give us time for a proper buryin'!'

'An hour,' Cole repeated. He settled the stetson on his head, and beneath the slanted brim, his features sat rigidly. 'I'm in command now and when I give an order, I'll expect it to be obeyed. Whoever can't live with that leaves the train. Understood?'

Nobody spoke. Nobody moved. In the tense hush, the slight soughing of the wind in the cottonwood assaulted their ears, and the faint, far-off call of a bird came clearly.

With the strength and suddenness that was so much a part of Cole McCullough, he swung into the crowd, the settlers falling back before him.

'You know what to do, now get going.'

They stared sidelong at him, casting glances of rebellion from the corners of lowered lids. They grumbled, muttering words of displeasure beneath their breath. But they obeyed. Heads bent, they moved off.

Cole turned to Leah.

'Once again—I'll take my gun.'

There was nothing in his face, his voice. Out of a night and morning of terror and tenderness, of small gentlenesses and searing anger, there was nothing. Less than nothing. It was with the indifference of a stranger that he regarded her.

Leah held out the revolver to him, and as he took it, she realised he had deliberately avoided touching her hand.

'I want you to know something, Miss Cabot. I helped you escape the renegade camp because I owed you a favour. I now consider that debt repaid. I've been entrapped against my will in leading this train West, and I'll show no one any special favours along the way. Including you.'

'I want you to know something as well, Mr McCullough,' Leah answered him swiftly, her ire rising with her words. 'I'll need no special favours to reach California! I made a promise to my grandfather at Fort Laramie that I would reach the Promised Land and build his school anew—and I intend to do just that!'

Cole made a small sound of contempt. 'Borrowed dreams!' He cast a hard glance towards the horizon. 'You can't go West with only the strength of borrowed dreams to sustain you. It's a brutal place and—and it needs a whole heart to tame it.'

Leah stared at him in something close to amazement. His words were her own feelings, buried so deep and hidden so well, she'd thought no one would ever discover them. 'How do you know that?' she demanded. 'How do you know those things?'

He lowered his eyes. 'I once knew a man who went West without dreams, and the West cut him in two.' Cole's voice lifted to scorn. 'Just like it's going to do to these poor innocent fools.' He shrugged and a cruel little smile crossed his face, heightening its harsh angularity. 'But then—it's not my place to care about that, is it? What were the terms of our agreement? Lead the train and live? It was never specified how many would have to make it.'

Leah stiffened, swallowing against her outrage, wounded by the words he had tossed away with such carelessness and more—the emptiness in his eyes. 'I know you're bitter about what happened today, but now that you've given us your word that you'll see us safely through—' She broke off helplessly. 'Surely you must feel some loyalty—?'

'Loyalty? For a passel of Yankees?'

Cole threw back his head and laughter crashed from his throat, the sound of it seeming to echo from the distant mountains, the mockery of it sweeping over her, even as the mockery of his laughter had swept over her during the battle. Even as it had that first, faraway morning, by the spring. Even as it had all the mornings and nights she had known him. Leah went white, and then hot blood darkened her face.

'I made my grandfather another promise,' she bit off, 'never to forget that it was the Southern rebels who ended his life, his dreams, and I never shall! Like all the others on this train, I'm tolerating the presence of a Confederate traitor simply because I want to reach California. I only hope persuading them to let you live wasn't a mistake!'

A cold smile spread wide beneath Cole's dark moustache. 'I wouldn't worry, Miss Cabot. If we don't reach the Promised Land, you can personally tie the rope around my neck.'

'I'd enjoy it!' Leah replied with a spite to match his own, but his expression didn't change. His smile, the look in his eyes, both were a casual stranger's still.

'The proper little Yankee—heading West on borrowed feelings, borrowed dreams.' He pushed up the brim of his stetson with a forefinger. 'It will be interesting to see if you make it.'

Cole turned on his heel and started away, and goaded, Leah shouted after him. 'I'll make it, Mr McCullough!'

He didn't stop, nor did he acknowledge her words, and looking after his retreating figure, Leah saw in the set of his broad shoulders, in the tilt of his head, a distance as great as that from North to South.

In his cool disinterest she read a challenge.

'I'll make it Mr McCullough,' she said again, but this time her voice was low, the words gritty with determination. 'I'll make it.'

CHAPTER
EIGHT

In every grinding turn of the wagon wheels, Leah heard the echo of Cole McCullough's challenge.

Heard it in the rushing of swift rivers, in the drone of insects, in the parching whisper of the endless wind. Heard it in the slogging steps of the oxen as they toiled up and down wearily winding foothills, in and out of deep-gullied ravines.

She saw it in the strange sight of Devil's Gorge, where violent water had carved a gate of stone. She read it in the inscriptions of mountain men and missionaries and trappers—the names of all those who had gone before, carved on the great, granite turtleback known as Independence Rock.

The challenge loomed in the grandeur of the Rockies, in the splendour of purple-sheened peaks rising up to snow-crested tops that pierced the very blue of the sky. And as the caravan battled through those mountains, the challenge lay in the women's weary eyes, in the men's slumped shoulders.

In her own aching body, Leah felt Cole McCullough's cool challenge born anew each day.

He drove them mercilessly.

He roused them well before sunup. He shortened the nooning, he lengthened the day's march. At night he had other orders. Every wagon was to be overhauled, every wheel greased, every canvas cover patched, and tacked with blankets or hides.

Every scrap of food was to be brought to the supply wagon, and he alone doled it out.

Every evening he portioned out the food. Every morning he seemed to awaken them a little earlier. Every day he seemed to push them a little harder.

It wasn't that he asked more of the others than he gave of himself. As if spurred by invisible demons, he drove himself the hardest of all. But even as he worked side by side with the others, righting an overturned rig, repairing a shattered axletree, hefting an axe, his labour was an empty thing, without camaraderie. He shared no trifling amusements, he gave no small encouragements. He spoke seldom, he never laughed, he seemed rarely to change his expression of hard aloofness.

And it was this, more than the orders and demands, they grated on the settlers. They wanted to see him as weary as they were. They wanted to see him drained and frustrated and fearful.

But as the days wore on and the miles mounted, there was no erosion in the rock wall that was Cole McCullough. His hard imperturbability was the goad under which the wagons moved. And watching ever, saying little—saying nothing—he led them into the desert.

As far back as Missouri, the settlers had heard stories of the Great Basin. Like a gunslinger with a notched Colt it had a reputation as a killer. And now every last one of them knew those stories to be true.

There was nothing ahead. Not a blade of grass, not a tree. Not a drop of water. There was only sky and baked clay, and the late August sun, burnishing white salt flats that had no beginning, no end.

The alkali glare singed the eyes, the alkali vapour poisoned the air and blistered the lips and seared the skin. The alkali dust, fine as ground glass, knifed into raw wounds. And over all—over everything—the heat. As if reflected up from some giant, seething cauldron, it hung on the horizon in shimmering waves.

Looking to that pitiless horizon, Leah passed a gritty arm over her forehead. Earlier in the day she'd been sticky with sweat, but after hours beneath the raging sun, she felt as if all the moisture had been broiled out of her.

Since they'd entered the desert, Cole had portioned out the water as well as the food, a cup at sunup, a cup at day down. Running a swollen tongue over parched lips, Leah tried not to think of the next ration. Quickly she cast a look to the silent figure beside her.

'How is Mr Simms, Birdie?'

Beneath her alkali-whitened hair, the woman's dusty face was etched with concern, for she had made the wagonmaster's fight her own. She shook her head. 'He's not good, Child. Mighty feverish—outta his head most of the time . . .'

Birdie's voice trailed off, and once again the only sound was the slow creaking of the wagon, wheels ever turning to the slogging rhythm of hooves fighting the sand.

Abruptly the grinding cadence halted, listlessly Blue sank in his traces. His thin flanks, where the bones showed like washboards, were heaving slowly, his eyes half-closed. In an instant both women were at his side, Birdie crouching in the sand to stroke his sun-flayed head.

'Git up, Blue,' Birdie urged in words softer than Leah

had ever heard her use. 'Please git up, boy—'

But from the saddle of the black gelding came a voice that scraped like flint against Birdie's gentleness.

'Cattle don't get up on the desert.'

Birdie lifted her head to plead with Cole. 'If he could have some extra feed, and some extra water, mebbe—'

'We all get our rations at the same time and in the same amount.' A muscle twitched in Cole's hard jaw. 'And starting today, we'll have to get along with less water. I'm cutting the ration in half.'

'But jest a mite of water, surely that couldn't hurt—'

'Don't beg him, Birdie!'

Fiercely, her hands on Birdie's shoulders, Leah drew the woman to her feet. Through lips stiffened with sand and pride, she said again, 'Don't beg him—not even for Blue!'

Cole didn't bend a glance on her. Not since the moment he'd left her beneath the gnarled cottonwood had he looked at her, and now his words were brief. 'I remember well enough you're not one for begging, Miss Cabot.'

'But I—I jest can't leave Blue to die alone—slowly—' Birdie's voice cracked, the brown hand on Blue's head trembling.

Cole drew his revolver. 'You won't need to.'

As Leah's lips parted in protest, he fired, and in the crack of the pistol she heard again his brutal words.

'When you've lived with death long enough, nothing—not even life—means anything to you.'

Cole turned his mount, holding up a gauntleted hand to halt the line of march, and every eye turned upward to the sun-bronzed man astride the black horse.

'From now on only those too sick to put one foot in

front of the other ride. Everyone else—' he dismounted, 'walks. And we walk day and night until we're out of the desert.'

He stood with feet spread wide in the sand, hands on his hips, and though his face was cold, closed in, Leah saw a strange flicker behind his amber eyes. Almost as if he were daring them to disobey.

But the caravan straggled on, the settlers toiling beside their wagons, and in its aftermath, Birdie and Leah lingered a moment, gazing at the still form of the gentle Blue.

He'd been a compatriot, a veteran of the same battles, he'd shared the same hardships. But his journey had come to an end. Slowly Leah's hand covered her lips, silently she wept. But Birdie merely whispered broken words.

'You low-down, good-fer-nothin', flea-bit, pea-brained critter—'

All that day, Birdie Gordon never looked back. But that night, as the howling of the coyotes fighting over Blue's carcass echoed hellishly down the trail, Leah heard her sobbing.

Steadily the settlers marched, day and night. After sundown the vast spaces of the desert held eerie strangeness, and the moon, hanging over all that emptiness, seemed too bright, too big—seemed to mock their efforts. But night was preferable to day, when the world became a broiling furnace and the sun poured molten lead on their heads.

Cole halted the caravan only for a short sunup rest and a briefer nooning that found most of them too weary to eat even the skimpy rations he allotted them. In heat-dulled stupors they would stand in line for their daily portion of water, their glazed eyes following too eagerly the movement of the ladle as he doled out their bare cupfuls. Then, stretching out ragged quilts in the scant shade of the wagons, they'd search for sleep.

But too soon the command would come.

'Move out!'

Too soon, too often, too hard, the orders came. And as the miles mounted and the days wore on—searing days, heat scorched miles—tempers wore like razors, honed to a cutting edge in the grinding sun.

It became impossible not to think of water.

Again and again Leah's mind wandered to the fountains that stood in Boston Common, to the blue of Boston harbour, to the Spring rain that had fallen against her bedroom window. She knew it was wrong, senseless torture, but she couldn't stop.

Once she had used water carelessly, now even a drop had become infinitely precious. She tried to imagine a whole barrel of it, pouring over her skin in wonderful, wonderful folds—

'Water!'

Had the word been born in the want of her own brain?

'Water!'

No! The shout was Sourdough's, and it had come from the crest of the small ridge ahead.

'It's water, folks! Sure as shootin'! Jest over the top of this hill!'

The settlers broke into a run, streaming after the fiddler, breasting the sands in eager, uneven strides to fling themselves face down at the edge of the pool. Leah, too, fell against the sand, her cupped hands, trembling with eagerness, reached out—

'The water's poisoned!'

Cole slammed his spurs into the gelding's flanks and slid to the ground, keeping one hand on the pommel, almost as if for support. Stretching out behind him, the marks of his horse's hooves left a path to the horizon. 'It's an alkali pool. Drink it and you'll go mad—or die.'

With palpable effort, the settlers pulled back from the deadly, tantalising glitter, the oxen bawling from the crest of the hill for water they would never taste.

Like an old woman, Leah drew up to her knees. Dully she stared into the pool. Strange . . . how anticipation could leave one with a need greater than before . . .

Sourdough's cracked voice sought hope. 'You been out scoutin', McCullough, jest when do you reckon we'll hit good water?'

Cole removed his hat and wiped the sweat from the band. Squinting towards the sunlight, he settled the stetson low on his forehead, and with a touch of irony, answered quietly, 'Unfortunately, I can't tell you that, Mr O'Rourke. Water holes dry up pretty fast around here.'

'Ya see what comes of trustin' a Johnny Reb!'

Still hunkered at the edge of the pool, Eb Hutter brought up his head, bugling his words against the brassy, mocking sunlight.

'McCullough was supposed to lead us outta this hell hole, but all he's led us to is poisoned water! Either he's lost the way or mebbe—mebbe he's done it deliberate.' A strange glint was born in Hutter's hooded eyes. 'Is that yer game, Reb?' he asked, spacing his words with menacing deliberation. 'Leadin' us in circles, hoardin' the water in that supply wagon you never let anyone see inside of—and when we drop in our tracks, havin' a proper party?'

The leaping of a muscle in his jaw his only betraying movement, Cole stared through Hutter. Crouched in the sand, the sodbuster taunted him again.

'If it ain't true, Reb, then show us the inside of that supply wagon. Come on—show us!'

Cole lunged forward. In both hands, he grabbed Hutter's shirtfront and yanked him to his feet. His voice was low but intense, and for the first time since assuming command, touched with something like emotion.

'I want you to shut your mouth, Hutter, and I don't want you to open it until we reach California.' With an abruptness that sent the sodbuster reeling, Cole loosened his hold. 'Now get moving!' He wheeled to face the others. 'All of you—get moving!'

They stared at him, suspicion grinding on faces already encrusted with bitterness. Their thoughts drummed almost loud enough to be heard.

Was he lost? Was he leading them to their destruction?

Through gritted teeth, Cole gave the order again, and in the silent desolation around them, his voice hung like death itself.

'Get moving!'

The amber eyes in the hard-edged face flayed them with a look cruel as the lash of a bullwhip, and in a ragged line they stumbled upright, staggering up the hill. On stiffened forearms, Leah struggled, too, to push herself aright. But the coin bright sun would not let her rise. Its rays forced her down, to her knees, then further still.

Dirty, thirsty, hopeless, she lay sprawled in the sand and thought of the old Leah Cabot. How clean and well-ordered she'd always been! How prim and dignified! Her gloved hands always folded before her as she walked sedately down the quiet streets of Boston, a bonnet always on her head to protect her skin from the sun.

Well . . . that girl was no more, her world gone as well. And gone, too, Leah knew, was her strength to seek another world. She'd struggled so long, she could struggle no more.

The shot that had killed Blue had killed something within her. Those borrowed dreams perhaps? Yes, yes, she'd lost them on this desert trail, even as Cole McCullough had said she would. California was a forever away and the now that she must endure to reach it was too much to be borne—so, like Blue, she would lie here and let the shifting sands cover her body. To cease fighting. To give up. It was all she wanted.

'Get up.'

Cole's voice stung her eyes open, and through dancing waves of heat she saw him. The homespun shirt he had lifted from a fallen renegade was black with sweat, his sun-seared, wind-burnt face shadowed with a stubble of beard, and unreadable. He seemed to sway as he stood over her, as if too weary to hold himself erect.

Or did he stand there at all?

The Cole McCullough she knew never weakened or wearied. This then must be but a desert mirage. She turned her head away, trying to dispel the image, but in a grip that hurt, Cole grabbed her shoulders and yanked her to her knees.

'I said get up!'

He took the canteen from his belt and held it out to her, but she pushed it feebly away. 'Leave me be,' Leah mumbled, 'let me alone.'

Lips drawing taut, Cole shoved the canteen into her hands, closing his own grip over hers, and rammed it to her lips.

'Drink, damn you!'

Leah glared at him, her black brows rushing together in a furious line. How she would hate this implacable man—if she had the strength to hate! He had no right to make her live! Violently she twisted free and grabbed away the canteen, overturning it. As a few drops of water spilled onto the sand, a small, triumphant cry broke from her blistered lips.

'Let me be or I'll spill the rest!'

Cole stared at the glitter on the ground, almost—unbelievable thought—as if he was as thirsty as she. Then he stepped back and lifted his head, and his eyes sparkled with sudden devilry.

'All right, Miss Cabot, lie here and die if you like. I've always known that beneath your brave words you were no better than the rest of these Yankees—a snivelling, white-livered coward!'

Spitting like an angry cat, Leah dropped the canteen and shot off the sand, all the suppressed fury of her feelings for Cole McCullough surging to life as she rushed at him. The torment she had suffered at his hands, the indignity, the yearning—they were festering sores, ground deep with desert dust, screaming for relief. With all the power she possessed, she slapped him across the face.

Choking on a sob, shaking, she drew back to strike him once more, but before his immobility she froze, arm upraised and trembling.

'Go on,' he said softly, 'hit me again.'

In the hot silence they faced one another. Leah could

hear his hard breathing, the harsh sunlight showing clearly the red mark of her hand against his cheek. She drew a long, shuddering breath, her body stilled, her hand dropped, and she was suddenly aware of a newly revived spirit.

The deadly torpor of sand and heat and bone weariness was gone—burnt away by anger and replaced by pulsing rebellion. And in that rebellion hope lived anew, hope stronger than the arid wastes around her, stronger even than the sun. Of course she would not die! Oh, no, she had no intention of dying!

Quickly she lifted the canteen. She brought it to her lips, letting a few swallows of the life-giving liquid slide down her throat, then handed it to Cole. Without a word, he turned, and in the path of his footsteps, Leah moved again to challenge the desert.

One foot in front of the other.

One foot in front of the other, Leah told herself. That's how they would make it to California. One foot in front of the other.

Don't reason, don't think. Only walk. Walk against the wind. Walk against the sand that sucked so treacherously at your feet—your spirit. Walk against the heat that played with pitiless abandon across your body.

Don't look at the oxen skulls and whitened bones that bordered the trail, the graves that stretched away on either side, pitiful reminders that not all who began this journey finished it.

Don't look at the buzzards circling overhead, ever watchful, ever waiting.

Only keep walking.

The world began to slip away from Leah, the edges of reality burning, blurring, unravelling . . . Faces faded into heat-soaked anonymity, time drifting from her like wisps of swirling sand. She had been travelling this road forever, this scorching road where the people plodded like ghosts, stupid with weariness.

But she kept walking. Kept looking to Cole Mc-Cullough.

He never slackened his pace, never rested. Never let them rest. Like the sun, he showed them no mercy.

Leah's hat fell to the desert floor, but she didn't retrieve it. Damp strands of thick hair straggled over her forehead, blinding her, but she didn't push them away.

She only kept walking. Kept looking to Cole Mc-Cullough.

Was that a break in the nothingness ahead?

Mustn't think—mustn't hope—

But the dark line grew, cutting into the horizon, slicing sand from sky. Could it be? Could it be? No, surely not. Any moment now the miracle would dissolve, splintering into bits of alkali.

But before their eyes, the thin line of hope stretched and widened and took shimmering form.

'Child,' Birdie breathed huskily, 'it's the river! It's the Truckee River! We've reached the river!' She fairly sang to the oxen. 'Mose! Buck! Duke! It's water, boys!'

But Birdie had no need to tell them—everywhere the drooping animals were lifting their heads, nostrils flaring in and out with the smell of water—clean, pure water. Their pace quickened to a trot, to a run, their harness chain ringing like bells. With the abandon of children, men and women kept gleeful pace beside the wagons.

Together, humans and animals stampeded for the river, the settlers dashing in while their teams drank their fill at the lapping edge. Leah waded in to her waist, rejoicing at the blessed coolness, while a sun that was no longer an enemy shone but lightly through the mesh of the cottonwoods, turning the water to silver. Birdie's laughter, the squeals of the children, the joyous shouts—all rose around her in mingled celebration.

Only one man stood apart.

Still on the bank, Cole stripped off his shirt with measured deliberateness. He plunged into the river, then straightened and shook off the water with the careless grace of a panther stretching in the sun.

Watching him, hating herself, hungry for the sight of him, Leah was agonisingly aware of the flash of white teeth against dark skin, stirred to the marrow by the play of muscles across his brown chest, by the breadth of his shoulders, the swell of his arms. The memory of that hard body pressed against her own was exquisite torture.

As if he felt the flame of her eyes, Cole turned his head, meeting her gaze. The colour shot to her cheeks, the blood beating fast in her throat, but she didn't turn away. For a long, heat-soaked moment they looked at one another, the shouts and sounds of the others fading—forgotten.

Once before they had shared such timelessness, Leah remembered, in the eternal darkness of a cave. And perhaps the world had hung in abeyance from that moment to this, for as she looked across the silvered water, she felt again that whisper of her womanhood, felt it winding throughout her body, stretching to all her senses, touching her with a weakness deep within.

And in that instant she recognised the real challenge that lay between them. That had hung forever between her heart and this man.

As if he realised it too, a corner of Cole's mouth

slanted up in a half-smile, speculative, surmising. Like a hunter with his quarry, he watched her.

Not now, his smile seemed to say, but soon, soon the challenge between us will be resolved.

The memory of that heat-drenched moment, that sun-bronzed man, filled Leah's day. It haunted her night.

While the rest of the caravan slept, she tossed and turned on the hard wagon bed, tortured with yearning, tormented with longing. A voice not of her own mind was calling out to her, a will stronger than her own was beckoning to her.

Desperately she sought the coolness of the river.

At the water's edge, within the tangled shelter of the cottonwoods, Leah knelt. All around her was stillness, but overhead the moon slipped in and out of scudding clouds, a prisoner of the disturbed sky, and as restless as she.

Leah buried her face in the water, then tilted back her head to let the drops thread down her arched throat, watched them trickle from between her upraised, interlaced fingers. She opened her shift, palming cool water against skin fired by desire.

But she found no relief.

Achingly she ran her spread hands down her shoulders, over her breasts, feeling that needling desire rise and pound within her. As on another night, a footfall sounded behind her. Slowly Leah turned.

And as she knew he would be, Cole McCullough stood waiting.

CHAPTER
NINE

IN the passing flare of the moonlight, his powerful silhouette held steady. His shirt hung open to the waist, sleeves rolled above his forearms, the stetson raked at an angle. Beneath the slanted brim, his gaze was rock hard, and at its insistence, Leah drew to her feet.

Like a fawn poised at the edge of a forest clearing, she faced him, full of trembling, as if she would flee at his slightest movement. The firm lines of her cheek and jaw were sculpted marble, and on the vivid face there was a soft glow, in the green eyes a wild shimmering. Her body was taut with need.

His hand closed over her wrist, and at his touch, she shuddered. A roaring began in her blood, a wanting—a wantonness. Slowly, deliberately, he pulled her to him, her back to his naked chest, her head to his shoulder. One arm he held across the weave of her hips, the other he pressed against her breasts, and over them both fell the cascade of her hair.

He began to caress her, running his hands over the contour of her body until she felt she could stand it no longer, until she felt his touch like flame through the thinness of her shift, singeing her skin. She was dizzy with the scent that clung to him, leather and wood smoke and sweat, intoxicated by that indefinable aura of his very masculinity.

'Tell me, Leah,' he commanded her, 'tell me why you came here tonight, why you sought me. Tell me why you called out to me in the cave—asked me to hold you.'

'I—I don't know—'

'You do know.'

There was a hot, driving note to his words, and as he turned her in his arms, she saw the heat of his voice in the amber eyes, a small, raw flame that burnt with a fierceness she couldn't understand.

'Tell me, Leah,' he said again, and his voice was hoarse, 'tell me—admit it. You want me, and you want me tonight.'

'No!'

Sudden, desperate effort ripped her from his arms, sent her to the edge of the lapping water. 'No! That isn't true!'

'Isn't it?'

In the lash of that voice, in the ferocity of the tawny eyes—and yes, most of all in the throbbing of her own body—Leah felt the power of his question.

Temples pounding, pulses drumming, she tried to fight down what cried for life within her, tried to cling to the tenets of her past. Utter obedience to her grandfather's word. Duty to his commands. Obedience—duty—Never forget his dream—Never forget your promises—But she could not think, could not remember. She fled into the river, seeking relief, a cooling of the searing crucible that was her body.

Quickly Cole was beside her. He swung her into his embrace, her head falling back across his arm.

'I know you, Leah, I know you better than you know yourself. You pretend a calmness like the surface of this water, but inside there's a wildness like all the rivers of the West.'

His mouth sought hers, his lips parting her own, his scalding kiss sending tremors through her soul. She writhed in agony, hot with shame, heady with desire.

He kissed her again, and this time his lips were slow and leisurely, raking her longing to an unbearable pitch. 'Please,' she moaned, the sound coming from deep in her throat. 'Please—' But was she begging him to cease—or never stop?

His head lifted. 'Say it, Leah, say it, you want me!'

Insistently his mouth hovered over hers, his will possessing hers utterly, the hot, leaping fire in his eyes burning her, purging her of all else but what she knew in her deepest heart.

Had always known.

'Say it, Leah—say it—'

'Yes,' she whispered, 'yes, I want you!'

Cole lifted her in his arms, and the rising of the wind in the cottonwoods was part of her own fierce desire. Confederate rebel? Gunman? It didn't matter. It never had. She was wild to belong to him. Wild as the raging rivers of the West . . .

She wound her arms around his neck, pressing the wet moulding of her body to his. Straining through her shift with drenched clarity, her breasts were crushed against his chest, her lips tasting the perspiration on his skin. And the thunder of his heart was the beating of her own.

As on that first night, when he'd carried her out of the bounds of her ordered life, so now he was carrying her out of mind—out of time.

And there was only the darkness and Cole Mc-Cullough and the wild insistence of her body.

On the soft, grassy bank he laid her down, leaning over her on straightened forearms. Then with one hand he drew aside the veil of her hair. 'You're not afraid?'

In answer, Leah pressed cupped hands to the hollows of his cheeks. The breeze was stirring the damp tendrils that clung to her temples, the restless moonlight spilling a soft, golden mist about her face and shoulders. Her eyes were luminous, body and soul vibrant with the need to give of herself to this man.

'Afraid?' she whispered. 'Not tonight—not ever again.'

Gently she pulled him down to her and their kiss held a completeness that wiped out the world. As if he could never have enough of her, Cole's lips travelled over her eyes, her mouth, her cheeks, her throat. Hungrily she answered him, returning kiss for kiss, caress for caress.

'Cole—' His name was a sob. 'Cole—I love you—'

His body tensed. He drew a rasping breath, then his hands ran beneath her flowing hair, tightening against her skull.

'So you love me, do you?' His voice erupted into gloating laughter. 'If all the Yankees had surrendered this easily, we would have won the war.'

All that was within Leah crumbled.

How cleverly he had set the trap, how easily she had walked into it. She had given him all of herself, holding back nothing, and he had taken her need and twisted it like a knife in a bleeding wound. He had won the challenge. Oh, yes—he had won the challenge. And more. He had vanquished her utterly.

Tears of hurt and humiliation scalded her cheeks and she tried to rise, consumed by shame. 'Please, Cole, please let me go—'

'Not just yet, Miss Cabot,' he whispered in words frighteningly soft—and in the sudden, demonic glitter of his eyes, she saw the black anger she had always feared, unbound and raging free.

Roughly his hands went to her shoulders, pinning her to the ground. He tore her shift, his hands moving across her body, against her bare flesh. Strong, brown hands, the black hairs growing thickly at the wrists, ruthless hands that caressed her uncaringly, bruising her. His mouth tore at her own, kissing her savagely, his brutal lips punishing the swell of her breasts, the tender, softly scented hollow between.

His kisses, his caresses—all seemed intended to wound her, degrade her, his arms tightening about her, crushing her until she cried out in pain.

With violent abruptness, Cole spun off the ground, standing with his back to her, his hands jammed into hard fists, as if he were straining at something within.

'Leave me,' he commanded her harshly, 'get back to the wagons!'

Leah struggled to her feet and fled—through the wildness of the thrashing trees, beneath the shadows of the troubled sky, into the fierceness of the stirring wind.

Insidiously that wind blew against her wet skin, wound through her violated body, chilling her to the soul. In vain she searched for something to warm her, searched for the old obedience, the old rules and regulations. Searched for her old life.

But all that was left to her were the threadbare rags of her torn pride.

The chill wind persisted.

It cooled the memories of the desert, it blew at the

ettler's backs, prodding them away from the river, owards the looming peaks of the Sierra Nevadas.

Gaunt, grim-faced, these mountains held a bleakness unlike the grandeur of the Rockies. They were a special world—a world unto themselves—a labyrinth of rocky error, of bare, soaring cliffs, of bald-faced summits that dropped away to nothingness.

But the Sierras must be scaled. For, like towering fortresses, they stood as sentries to the Sacramento Valley. Only by their gates did one enter the Promised Land.

The single way through was Truckee Pass.

Upward, ever upward, the settlers wound towards that sheer channel of hope. The tall towers of the mountain peaks cast long shadows over their path, the craggy reaches overhead arrogantly shouldering the sky, scorning their strength—challenging them.

Or was the challenge Cole McCullough's still?

He permitted them only a day at the river when they might have used a month. He gave the oxen no respite as they hauled the wagons up the pine-forested slopes, ordering them double teamed rather than allowing them to rest—ordering the men to scrape free the ridged trail from rock slides, ordering the women to hack away the brush. When the grade grew too steep, he commanded the wagons eased down by ropes.

Trailworn, dull-eyed, the settlers finally bedded down in sight of the Pass—and for that night, their weariness was forgotten. Soon—soon they would see the fertile valley of the Sacramento, see its velvet grass and sapphire lake. Soon they would see the Promised Land!

But the wind that had brought a chill to the lowlands carried a special curse to the upper trails. Winter came

early in the mountains, and the snow that already glis-
tened on the ridges overhead was an ominous prediction
of the future. That night the storm began.

By the next afternoon the wagons were already wal-
lowing through heavy drifts, the oxen straining against
their hickory yokes, deep, sloughing tremors shaking
their emaciated bodies. In woollen sack coats, blankets
about their shoulders, the settlers slogged beside their
teams. When the children could climb no longer, the
parents hefted them in their arms, and heads down
against the ever-thickening curtain of the sky, pelted by
snow and sleet, the caravan inched on.

Time and again Cole led the assault on the Pass. Time
and again they tried.

Strain a foot forward . . . hands too numb to feel the
harness chains . . . tug at a wheel, push at the wagon, the
snow slapping the oxen's bellies . . . tramp a passage
through the drifts . . . hour after hour. Try again—and
again. And fail.

'Lighten the wagons!'

From the saddle of the black gelding, Cole's new
order rang down the line. 'Lighten the wagons! Only
ammunition, tools, and a few necessities will be allowed!
Lighten the wagons!'

Feeble dissent drifted up. They had endured the
plains, lived through the desert, they had given so
much—must they give over even this last? These final
few links with their old lives? But their protests went
unheeded by Cole McCullough—and slowly, the scrap
heap of memories grew.

Claw-foot tables and crates of china. Rocking chairs
and sheet-iron stoves and silverware and butter churns.
Remnants of the generations. Fragments of the past.

All—all of it tossed beside the trail. The bits and pieces of so many lifetimes . . . silently buried by the falling snow.

Within the wagon bed, Leah ran cold chapped hands over the well-worn leather of her grandfather's trunk. How carefully she had packed it all those months ago. She lifted the lid and passed a fleeting caress over the array of books. A Latin text. *Memoirs of Aaron Burr*. Shakespeare. James Fenimore Cooper. Ralph Waldo Emerson. Dickens. Poe. And more.

Leah slammed the lid shut. She slid the trunk to the edge of the wagon, then hefted it to her shoulder. Straining under its weight, she carried it to the very edge of the slope. With a vengeance she heaved it over the side.

She could not see its passage, but she could hear it. Like the lurching of a dead man, it pounded its way to the bottom of the gorge. Then—silence.

'You hauled that trunk clear from Boston, child—I know it's a hard thing we been called to do, give away our treasures—'

From behind Leah, Birdie's awkward voice fell away, but resolutely, her footsteps battled a path through the snow. 'I—I reckon yer sayin' goodbye to yer Grandpa all over again.'

Leah shook her head. The wet sleet, stinging her eyelashes, knifing her cheeks, felt like tears. But she'd shed all her tears long since, running through the fury of a wind-swept night, the very core of Leah Cabot fading into nothingness with the retreating sound of her footsteps. Now her eyes were dry and hard—like her voice.

'I'm saying goodbye to his dream, Birdie.'

'I'm mighty glad to hear that, child!' Within the

weathered face, Birdie's eyes snapped with blue intensity, and firmly she took hold of Leah's shoulders. 'Now you can find a life of yer own—a dream of yer own!' She nodded upward, towards the soaring cliffs, but their arrogance didn't quell Birdie Gordon.

'Old Jim Bridger made it through that Pass—Kit Carson, too! A heap of them mountain men made it through—and we will, too! Oh, not without a little sweat, but any dream worth havin' is worth fightin' fer! And when we do—' her voice softened to clumsy gentleness, 'why, you'll find that dream of yer own in the Promised Land!'

With a final tightening reassurance of her hands, the woman turned, tramping her way back to the wagon. Leah watched her go, then lifted her gaze to the snow-choked skies. How to explain?

How to explain that once she'd stood on another hill, a lowland hill, overlooking Fort Laramie, and standing there, had tasted the ashes of remembrance and accepted a borrowed dream as all she'd ever have?

How to explain that once, on the tree-sheltered banks of a river, she'd denied that dream and all that John Cabot had made her, and watched, dying inside, as the wind blew away forever all that she might have become?

Against her will, Leah turned her eyes to the dark man astride the black horse. The collar of his jacket was turned up, the brim of his stetson slanted down, and in the amber eyes was a hardness as unrelenting as the dark line of the mountains. As chill as that wind that had ripped the hope from her hands and scattered it like the broken shards of her heart.

How to explain that the Promised Land held no dreams for Leah Cabot?

        *   *   *

Steadily, dreadfully, the snow kept falling. For two days more, the settlers—at Cole McCullough's orders—hurled themselves against it. But their failing strength was no match for the fury of a mountain blizzard, and on the second night, huddled around the campfire, hunched over their plates, their silence was a desperate thing.

'Fiddler!' Birdie bellowed abruptly. 'Play us a tune—that's what we need!'

Sourdough shot her a glance. Ice clung to his divided whiskers, and his eyes were teary with cold, but his temper was still blazing. 'Dang females! Never kin let a man have a mite of rest—'

'Shut up and play,' Birdie interrupted complacently.

The whitened wisps of Sourdough's grumbling breaths drifted upward as he pulled off his gloves and blew on his fingers. As he reached beneath his coat, the settlers discovered why the folds had hung so bulkily on his skinny frame—tenderly they had cradled fiddle and bow.

> From this valley they say you are going,
> We will miss your bright eyes and sweet smile;
> For they say you are taking the sunshine
> That has brightened our pathways awhile.

Sourdough's raspy voice hung long in the darkness, and moving against the bittersweet sound of his music, Leah stirred from her place by the fire. Quietly she offered her plate to Mrs Hutter.

'For the children.'

The woman looked quickly up, conscience warring with her family's need. Daily the food Cole allotted them had dwindled, until now a few dried apples and a slice of fried cake—no more than flour and water this, with the consistency and taste of glue—had to suffice for a day.

'Miz Cabot, I can't take yer ration! I know you been givin' away yer food, and all last night you tended to them that's taken ill with the cold, and the night before, too! Never eatin', never sleepin', yer gonna take sick yourself—'

Firmly Leah pressed the plate into Mrs Hutter's hand, stilling her protests. With unspoken gratitude, the woman accepted the gift.

Tugging her shawl more firmly about her head, wrapping her arms about her body, Leah pulled away from the fire's flare. Hunger? Weariness? She no longer knew what those meant. Leah Cabot had gone past the needs of the living.

> Come and sit by my side if you love me,
> Do not hasten to bid me adieu,
> Just remember the Red River Valley
> And the cowboy who loved you so true.

Leah shivered. The scraping of the fiddle was the refrain of her own inner barrenness . . .

'Leah—'

She stiffened at the sound of Cole's voice, tautening her muscles as if preparing for battle. Very still she stood, telling herself that soon, soon her congealed breath would loosen, telling herself that the flood of feeling welling within was wrong for someone who was dead.

'Turn around, Leah,' he said quietly, a note in his voice she had never heard before.

She dropped her arms to her sides, her head lifting, her jaw tightening. Back straight—defiance in every soft-curving line of her—she obeyed him. Lightly his hands came to her shoulders, his nearness driving daggers through her. Why—why didn't he go and leave her in peace? Why did he need to torment her further?

With a strange intensity he studied her face, and in the dim light of the snow-filled sky, his amber gaze held something she couldn't understand, a pleading almost— a searching. A hoping.

'Leah—' he said again, a breaking in his voice, as if that single word held all the pain in her own heart.

What a fool she was! His vulnerability was but a trick of the night shadows. His words, the look in his eyes, but a reflection of her own suffering. The pain was hers— and always had been.

Well, never again would she walk willingly into his trap.

'Take your hands from me,' she said steadily, deliberately, cruelly. 'And never—for any reason—touch me again.'

She was amazed at the pitilessness of her own words. But why not, she thought bitterly? She'd learned from a master.

He jerked away, half-turning, then abruptly, he spun around and swept her close, crushing his lips against hers.

Leah made no effort to resist him, but only stood woodenly in his embrace. Beneath his kiss, her mouth was indifferent. He had no way of knowing it took actual physical effort for her to remain passive in his arms. The effort of a lifetime.

His grip tightened, and she could feel the tremor of

those arms as he pressed her head against his shoulder, his tormented eyes willing her, it seemed, to respond. But she gave nothing.

His hands dropped. He stood away from her, and for a moment more, Leah forced her body rigid, kept that cool, untouched mask on her face until a kind of understanding dawned in his eyes. He turned. And in the wake of his going, Leah put out a hand to steady her trembling.

> They will bury me where you have wandered,
> Near the hills where the daffodils grow,
> When you're gone from the Red River Valley,
> For I can't live without you I know.
>
> Come and sit by my side if you love me,
> Do not hasten to bid me adieu,
> Just remember the Red River Valley
> And the cowboy who loved you so true.

Cole strode to the fire. With one boot, he kicked a cloud of snow into the flames, and his voice was raw against the wind, halting Sourdough's singing.

'Get back to your wagons! You'll need all your strength for the days ahead.'

Eb Hutter snapped his long body upright. 'You've been workin' us like horses every step of the way since Wyomin', McCullough! But I've taken my last order from you, Reb!' He smashed his tin plate against a rock protruding from the snow. 'And I've eaten all of this slop I'm goin' to! It's our food you been hoardin'—and I mean to git my share!'

Without warning, the sodbuster whipped a knife from

beneath his coat. He dove for the supply wagon—and in a single, wicked thrust, slashed open the canvas cover.

The wagon was empty.

Hutter went pale. 'There's nothin'—nothin' left—'

'You're right,' Cole answered him evenly, 'there's nothing.'

A child's frightened sobs shook the night, the mother's answering 'Hush,' laced with an equal fear. For so long there had been so little. And tomorrow there would be less.

'We trusted you, Mr McCullough,' Emma Rance said softly. 'We trusted you to look properly to our supplies.'

'You lousy Johnny Reb!' Hutter's hands curled into claws. 'You made us give over every bit of our food to you—and now we're trapped in the snow without a scrap! We won't last a week!'

'Mebbe—mebbe if we went huntin',' Caleb Rance cast out hopefully—desperately. 'Mebbe that would help some—'

'Appears like McCullough's been huntin',' Sourdough said dryly. He motioned with his bow to the pack mule that stood tethered · in the shadows, bereft of bounty. 'I reckon game's a mite scarce now.'

'Tomorrow we shoot one of the oxen,' Cole said without emotion. 'We'll live on that as long as we can.' He· pivoted, starting away, but Rance clutched at his arm.

'But if we kill the animals,' the little miner questioned shakily, 'how do we haul the wagons to California?'

'Ain't none of us gonna make it to California,' Hutter spat out. 'We're dead—all of us. Dead.' He rounded on Cole, the grinding of his boots against the snow the sound of his intent, his hooded eyes the gleaming reflection of the knife he twisted in bony fingers.

'We had a deal, Reb,' he said thickly, 'you lead us to California, we let you live. Well, it don't look to me like you've kept yer part of the bargain.' He thrust the knife savagely forward, grazing the air between them, and his voice took on the biting menace of his blade. 'Don't look that way at all!'

Cole's hand shot to his revolver and came up lightning fast as he dropped to a ready crouch. Fear dropping his mouth, Hutter stumbled backward.

Cole didn't move, didn't speak. The tawny eyes narrowed, a muscle in his jaw twitching. Very slowly he straightened. His gun hand dropped, the revolver slipped to the ground.

'You can shoot me in the back, Hutter, it'll save you the trouble of a hanging.'

Cole swung into the shadows, and as he went, a hand to the heart she thought would tear through her breast, Leah saw that his heavy shoulders were bent, his head bowed, his once hard body gaunt with strain. A blast of frigid mountain air ripped around the edges of the camp, sending her gasping before it—its very violence seeming to tear the scales from her eyes, clearing her vision.

She had thought Cole McCullough invulnerable, but she'd been wrong. He was weary unto death. And why not? His strength had carried them all for these weary months.

She took a faltering step forward, but the wind drove her back, her own remorse holding her frozen.

She'd thought that Leah Cabot had grown strong on her own, but she'd been wrong about that, too. As far back as the night she'd faced down Two Hatchet, it had been that rock wall of Cole's strength she'd braced her back against—his bravery fuelling her own.

It had been Cole who'd carried her from a room of death and brought her solace. It had been Cole, enduring the sting of the lash for her sake, leading her from a night of endless horror. It had been Cole who'd spared Blue the agony of a slow death when neither she nor Birdie had had the courage. It had been Cole who'd bullied her into life on the desert.

It had been Cole—giving her his water ration.

And all during the days and nights of that endless march through the sand, it had been Cole's stamina she'd drawn on—his strength becoming her own.

Again and again.

But tonight, when for the first time he'd come to her, pleading as much as a man like Cole McCullough could plead, seeking a refuge, she'd turned him away.

The chains dropped from Leah's feet and she began to run. The snow dragged at her steps, but she didn't care, the sleet cut at her face, but she didn't notice. She only knew that she must reach Cole.

But she had forgotten Eb Hutter.

A shot rang out. Cole swayed on his feet—and as he crumpled to the ground, Leah heard once again her name on his lips.

CHAPTER
TEN

SOMEHOW the others were gone—had it been Birdie who'd ushered them away? Had it been Birdie as well who'd brought water and bandages and blankets? Leah didn't know. Her only conscious thoughts were of Cole—and a fleeting awareness of Eb Hutter, of the befuddled look in his eyes as he stared down at the man he'd shot.

'I'm sorry—so sorry,' he mumbled again and again, until pale and shaking he had no more words and the muscles of his jaw hung slack. The bile of his tortured hate had been lanced, the draining bitterness leaving but the pathetic dregs of a man, disintegrating before her eyes.

Like a mother with her child, gently, firmly, Abigail Hutter took her husband's arm. 'My Eb was a different man before the war . . . Somethin' happened to him when he was fightin'—when he heard our boys was dead . . .'

Leah watched the woman lead her shambling husband towards their wagon, then all else was wiped away before the need to tend to Cole.

Eb Hutter's unsteady aim had resulted in but a flesh wound to the shoulder, and carefully Leah bathed and bandaged it. But more than the wound, it was fatigue that had sent Cole reeling. Drawing his head in her lap, covering him with blankets, she let him sleep on.

Sometime in the past moments the snow had stopped
. . the world was still, crisply clear, solitary. In the pale
light of the moon and stars, Cole's face was drawn tight
over the angular bones, his brow furrowed. Even at rest
his inward struggle raged. With a gentle hand, Leah
smoothed back the hair from that creased forehead.

Slowly his eyes opened.

'I thought you were a dream,' he whispered huskily,
'like that first night, when I opened my eyes and saw you
bending over me.' He reached up a hand to the curling
wisps of hair straying from beneath her shawl, then let
his touch roam the curve of her cheek. 'Your hair was
loose, falling over your shoulders, and your eyes were so
soft . . . You were the most beautiful thing I'd ever seen
in my life—'

He pushed sharply upright, a grimace of pain grazing
his face, one hand going instinctively to his shoulder.
'You were the first decent thing I'd seen in so many
years—'

'Cole!'

Soft as the fragrance of flowers, yet throbbing with
insistence, Leah's voice moved through her unsteady
breathing. 'Cole,' she said again, 'tell me about those
lost years! Tell me—everything!'

Clenching and unclenching his powerful hands, he
loomed over her. He drew an audible breath.

'All right,' he said finally. 'All right.'

He walked a few steps past her and raised one booted foot to a wagon wheel. Tilting back his head, he
searched the skies, as if the biting night beauty held
some strange secret.

'Vermillion . . . that was the name of our plantation.
In north Georgia it was. "Best damn cotton country in

the world," my father used to say—and he was right
After the Spring rains, the rolling hills would be red—
blood-red, waiting for the cotton seeds . . .'

His voice trailed off, resuming with a lilting resonance
that caught Leah in its spell, so that she, too, saw past the
present, through the mountain snows to that Georgia
Spring.

'I can see it all—just as it used to be! The white pillars
the gardens, blooming with dogwood, the avenue o
oaks, the winding road that ran through the pine forest
down to the river. I can see my mother, sitting on the
verandah, hear the rustle of her hoops, smell the flower
in her hair. How she loved to dance! The balls she gav
at Vermillion! My father preferred the hunt to waltz
ing—he raised me in the saddle! He saw to it that
excelled at everything a Georgia gentleman should—
riding well, drinking hard, shooting straight.'

Like the key to some distantly imagined world, hi
bittersweet words held Leah entranced, opening he
eyes to Cole McCullough as he must have been. Boote
to the knee, clad in a scarlet coat and fashionabl
breeches, the sleek, careless kind of man Grandfathe
John had always thundered against.

'And then the war came.'

Spring was gone. Winter had returned to his voice.

'I killed my first man at Manassas—I watched his fac
twist in agony as he died. I watched my men fall . . . on
by one . . . Day after day I heard their screams. Th
killing never stopped. Antietam. Chancellorsville
Fredericksburg. Shiloh. The river ran red with blood a
Shiloh! Day after day I saw death and inflicted deat
until the dying had no more faces—'

His words went on and on, low, swift, hot words

agonised words, wrenched from within. Fists clenched, teeth gritted, sweat streaming down his face despite the cold, his words spilled forth, pouring out poison.

The pain in his voice, the searing anguish on his face, tore Leah in two. She couldn't bear to watch, couldn't bear to listen, but she must watch, she must listen. She must let him vent all the bitterness he'd been harbouring, so that at long last he would be free of it.

'I saw fields heaped with the dead—men dumped into mass graves like so many sacks of flour. And the wounded—rows and rows of mangled men, their faces shot away, guts hanging out, their flesh rotting on their bodies—I won a medal for bravery at Chancellorsville. Bravery!' He threw back his head and roared with laughter; Leah shivered at the sound of it. 'To be brave you have to feel fear, and I felt nothing. Death didn't frighten me. Death was an old friend.

'Fight, march, retrench. Fight, march, retrench. Day after day. Fight, march, retrench—and fight again. And still the Yankees came—more and more! The cannons were never silent—our hands were always red with blood—' He stretched out rigid palms, as if he saw still those bloody stains. 'But the worst was Gettysburg.'

Gettysburg! In a rush of memory, Leah heard again the grey strangeness of Grandfather John's voice, saw again the casualty list flutter to the floor. Read again the name of Lieutenant Micah Cabot. And Cole McCullough had been there, too.

Cole dropped to a knee beside her, face taut, eyes blazing, and Leah knew he no longer saw her. He was riding to a battle long since over, fighting a war long since lost.

'We were ordered to fall in with Pickett's division—

charge the Union lines at the very centre! I shouted orders at my men until I was hoarse, but I couldn't save them. They were mowed down like a field of ripe wheat. They looked to me for help, but I couldn't give them any—'

Faster yet his words came, nearly incoherent in their frenzy, his eyes wide and unblinking. In a bone-wrenching grip he seized Leah's hand, pulling her into the maelstrom of his nightmare. And though silent tears streamed down her face, she held his gaze unwaveringly.

'I was shot off my horse—they found me on the field in a tangle of bodies—they thought I was dead, too. The medics tossed me in a cart piled high with corpses—all day I lay there, smelling death, feeling death—'

He stopped and passed a shaking hand over his forehead, and then came heavily to his feet. When he spoke again his low voice was wiped clean of all feeling, the absence of emotion more dreadful than any violence could have been.

'One of the burial squad heard me moaning, pulled me out. The Yankees patched me up and sent me West with a contingent of prisoners—they were desperate for men to fight the Apaches. We built a Fort in the middle of nowhere, the blue bellies driving us like dogs in the desert heat.' His words broke on a bitter laugh. 'Human cattle were far easier to replace than their mules and pack horses. We worked—and we fought. I learned a different kind of fighting out there, how to slit a man's throat in the darkness, how to split a skull with a hatchet. We worked like animals and we fought like animals until everything fine and decent—everything human—was ground out of us and we became animals.

'When the surrender came, they opened our cages and

turned us loose with a horse and a gun. I rode like a
madman back to Georgia—back to Vermillion.' He
drew an unflinching breath. 'But General Sherman had
already been there, on his march to the sea. My home
was a pile of rubble—my mother dead in the fire that had
destroyed it. My father— My father had died defending
Atlanta. Greybeards, little cadets from the Military
Academy, prisoners from the state penitentiary—they'd
all been called out to fight Sherman. They marched
together—and they died together. The scent of death
was all over Georgia . . .'

His voice died out and his mouth curved upward, into
a rigid smile brimming with self-mockery. 'Cole McCullough, sole heir of one of the wealthiest planters in the
state, and all I had to my name was a gun. And all I
remembered how to do was kill. I decided to return
West, put that gun out for hire. But I was bushwhacked,
the few things I had stolen. I'd sunk so low I didn't think
I could sink any lower, it didn't seem to matter what I
did. So . . . I decided to try robbery to get back my
stake. And then—'

He paused, and that pause pulsed long in the
shrouded night. He turned a hard gaze to Leah. 'And
then I found you. Leah,' he went on stiffly, 'I've loved
you since the moment I first looked into your eyes.'

All of Leah stilled. Barely breathing, waiting, wanting, longing to caress him, she searched for a word—a
look—that would give her leave to come to him. But he
only stood across the expanse of snow and watched her.
Unapproachable—even now.

In a flash of the old, sudden savagery, Cole kicked out
at the smouldering embers of the fire, sending a shower
of red sparks upward, into the night.

'I loved you,' he said again, a driving pain to his words, 'and I hated you! You made me feel again, and I'd thought I was done with feeling. You brought me back from the grave—and all I wanted was to stay dead. The closer you came to breaking through my shell, the more I had to hurt you, torment you! I had to drive you away—or go half-crazy from wanting you! I—I think I did go a little mad after I left you at Fort Laramie. I was running away—and I knew it. Running away from my feelings for you, even while I was trying to grab at a last chance for something that I knew was long gone.'

His voice fell to no more than a hoarse whisper. 'You don't know how I felt—watching you walk towards me in that cave—when I thought I'd never see you again. Yet knowing I couldn't come to you, couldn't touch you. I could have killed Pierce Greville with my bare hands when he hurt you—'

Cole broke off, a haunted look coming into his eyes. 'It was even harder after that, keeping myself away from you. I had to tell myself over and over that you were a Yankee, just to keep my hate alive! But no matter how I tried to drive you from my heart, Leah . . . you were always with me!'

Leah could wait no longer. Face dappled with moonlight, vivid with love, she stretched out her arms to him, ready to give all, to spare nothing. But abruptly Cole swung away from her.

'Don't add to my torment,' he said in a ragged voice. 'There is more you must hear. When I was forced to take command of the wagon train, it was like—like the war all over again. So many looking to me for their very lives! Old feelings, old pain made new—it all came back to me.

'I knew how low the supplies were, how little time we

had before they ran out, but I couldn't let the others know. It would have destroyed all hope. So I rationed the food. I knew how near the oxen were to the end of their endurance, so I ordered everyone to walk—lightened the wagons.

'I knew we had to get through the mountains before we were trapped by the first snows—we'd lost precious time at Laramie! So I kept pushing—kept driving—I couldn't let myself break, not once, not with so many people depending on me—'

The tautness drained from his body, his shoulders bent. 'But I've failed you—all of you—like I failed my men. It was that I wanted to tell you tonight, Leah. I wanted to hold you in my arms and tell you I had no strength left. I needed you, Leah, even though I had no right.'

'You had every right!'

The earth heaving strangely beneath her feet, Leah stood. Strange, spotty darkness danced a moment before her eyes, misting the world, but impatiently she brushed it aside. A visible pulse was beating in the deep hollow at the base of her throat and she swayed slightly in her intensity.

'Cole—' her tone was rich, freighted with compassion, 'let me be your strength!'

He snapped quickly around, the colour draining from beneath his tan. 'My strength,' he repeated incredulously. 'Leah, you're my heart and soul, my life—' He started towards her, then suddenly, clenching his hands into fists with the effort, he checked himself.

'That night at the river,' he said fiercely, 'I wanted you so much I would have taken you then and there, but when you said you loved me, I realised how little I had to

offer. God! It was the blackest moment of my life, that's
why I lashed out at you. Wanting you—loving you!—but
knowing I must never claim you— Don't you see? The
war left me a broken man, a man without hope, without
dreams. All I know, all I have left is hate—'

His tawny eyes darkened, glittering with tormented
lights, and in their depths, Leah saw the embittered gaze
of the dying John Cabot. She saw the dancing, dark
gleam of Pierce Greville's madness—the lost bewilderment of Eb Hutter. All of them robbed of their dreams
by battlefields that stretched from Bull Run to Appomattox.

But she would not let the war claim Cole McCullough!
His salvation hung in the balance and she was prepared
to fight for it.

Any dream worth having is worth fighting for, Birdie
had said, and she would fight for Cole McCullough's
dream! For his dream and her own. For her dream *was*
the dark, tortured man who stood before her.

Across the oddly rocking earth, Leah came to him, all
of her being concentrated in her eyes. 'Cole, you must
believe me, you must listen to me! Together we can find
a new life—I know we can! Together we can find a new
dream!'

And then, at last, the shelter of his strong arms came
around her and there was dawning wonder in his voice.

'Yes, Leah, yes! Together we can find that new life—'

Sweet, dizzying joy sang through Leah. She reached
the tips of slim fingers to the face that was wavering so
strangely, so darkly before her. She felt as if she were
falling—falling—but she didn't worry, for Cole's arms
were tight around her.

Why she should suddenly be so overwhelmingly

weary, she did not know, but before she gave way to that weariness, she must—must tell him one last thing—

'Cole, our love is stronger than hate . . .'

She was trapped in the desert, running endlessly through the burning wastes, her body a pillar of fire. Yet she went on, running and searching—

But why was she running and for what was she searching?

Cole. Of course, that was it. She was searching for Cole.

Where was he? Where was he?

Once she thought she'd found him, slumped in the sand. But when she came closer, it was the mad face of Pierce Greville that gleamed up at her . . .

And then she was no longer on the desert, but fighting her way across a death-strewn battlefield, as cold as she had been hot, her teeth chattering. But still she searched on, running through a field running red with blood. She saw the silent, staring corpses of Grandfather John and Micah and Eb Hutter, but she pressed on, for she must save Cole from death.

All at once she saw him, far, far away. She tried to call his name, but her cry was only a whisper. The cold was gone, as the heat before it, but now she was so weary she could barely take a step. Yet she forced her aching limbs forward—for she must reach Cole before death swallowed him up—took him from her forever.

But just as she neared him, his face shifted and slipped away, and became Birdie's.

'Birdie—?' Leah questioned weakly.

'Yer darn tootin', it's Birdie!' The woman snuffled loudly. 'Thank the good Lord—yer fever's broken.'

'Fever,' Leah echoed blankly. Dazedly she looked about her. She was in the wagon, covered with a blanket, a pillow beneath her head. 'Have I—have I been ill?'

Birdie blinked. 'Have you been—' She blew out her cheeks in disbelief. 'Child, you been outta yer head fer nigh unto five days—and I don't mind tellin' you, I was plum worried! Took sick with trail fever, you did, and it's no wonder, wearin' yerself out tendin' to the others.'

Delirious for five days? But— Desperately Leah groped for remembrance until once more she was standing in a snow-misted night, in the shelter of Cole's arms. 'How did I get here, Birdie? The last thing I remember was—was—'

'Mr McCullough carried you here, child.' In the blue depths of Birdie's eyes there was understanding, and quiet knowing. 'He lit out that same night, said he was gonna get you help—or die tryin'. And I'll be dad-gummed if a rescue party didn't get here yesterday! From one of the trapper's outposts they come, loaded with food and medicine. It was the quinine pulled you through, child, and it's the vittles gonna give you the strength to go on—give us all the strength to go on.'

A grim smile stretched Birdie's faded lips taut. 'Thanks to Mr Cole McCullough, we're all gonna live to see the Promised Land! I'll tell you, Child, folks are startin' to understand why Mr McCullough did things the way he did—startin' to see past the uniform he used to wear to the man inside. There's not a soul on this train won't remember him kindly—'

Swiftly Birdie caught herself, but not before sudden, dreadful suspicion welled in Leah's eyes. She struggled to a sitting position, throwing off her blankets, possessed by a fear so great she could not force it to her lips—the fear of her delirium, come to life.

'Cole,' she murmured frantically, 'I must find Cole—'

But Birdie's gentle hand on her wrist stayed her, and in the woman's brief words was the ringing of a death knell.

'The rescue party was set on by Injuns, Cole stayed behind, to head 'em off—so's the supplies could git through. Child—he didn't come back.'

CHAPTER
ELEVEN

ONE week later the caravan stood ready to roll.

Under a morning sun that had begun to melt the snow from the Pass, beneath a wind blowing light as spindrift, the settlers waited by their wagons. Yet unlike a morning miles and months ago, they stood quietly, no longer looking to the Western horizon with adventurous eyes.

No longer did their rigs sparkle white, the canvas covers as patched and stained as their clothes. No longer did their teams stamp eagerly in the traces, the oxen as trail-weathered as their masters.

And changed, too, was the man who faced them. Alonzo Simms had resumed command after Cole's departure, and though mended, the morning sun found him still a bit unsteady on his feet, his big frame wasted, jowls hanging loose, ruddy skin faded to a putty colour. Yet he jutted out the big jaw with the old determination as he began speaking.

'I got me a few things to say this mornin', and the first is 'bout Mr Cole McCullough.'

A shudder shook through Leah's body, slender as a willow wand after her illness. She clenched her hands at her sides, as if anchoring herself for the words to come, and watching her, Birdie's features creased into worry. She sighed heavily, all her frustrations of the past days in that sound, for Leah had steadfastly refused comfort.

'I know we all been hopin' McCullough would show up one of these days.' The wagonmaster shook his head. 'But it don't look like he's gonna make it—and we can't afford to wait another day. Our stock is rested, we're all tolerably fit—and most important, the Pass is as free of snow as it's gonna be till Spring. From now on, the weather will only be gettin' worse—there's no tellin' when another blizzard will hit! We got to go today.'

Simms drew a heavy breath, shifting his weight from foot to foot, the strain of his effort beginning to tell. 'And the truth of it is—I don't think McCullough would want us to wait any longer! He stayed behind so we could find a new life in a new land! He stayed behind so we could go on! And it seems to me, that if we don't want what Cole McCullough did to go fer nothin', that's what we gotta do—go on! To California!'

The wagonmaster stopped and his eyes went quietly around the circle. One by one heads came up, shoulders straightened. Yes, the trail had changed every one of them, but though it had battered them, it had not broken them. From hardship had come a grit fiercer than anything they'd imagined in Missouri.

From a man's courage had come the strength to finish their journey.

With a spirit as unconquerable as the golden land that awaited them, the settlers gave back the wagonmaster's gaze.

But Alonzo Simms was not quite done. 'Now the next thing I got me to say is—well—I been in some pretty bad scrapes before, but that arrow in my belly was the narrowest squeak I ever had! It's only because of Birdie Gordon that I'm here right now—and—well—' He jabbed at his sombrero, he took it off and put it back on, and removed it once more. 'What I'm tryin' to say is—well—'

'Aw shoot!' Impatiently Birdie stumped forward. 'I'll tell 'em! As soon as we hit California, me and this big buffalo are gettin' hitched, leastways, I think we are.' Sudden suspicion narrowing her eyes, Birdie glared up at Simms. 'It wasn't the fever that made you propose, was it?'

As laughter exploded through the company, the wagonmaster grinned down at the peppery little woman who came barely up to his shoulder. ''Course it wasn't!' He wagged his head. 'Birdie Gordon, you are the dog-gonedest female!'

'Yer losing a good woman, O'Rourke,' Emma Rance gibed at the fiddler, elbowing him in his skinny ribs. But Sourdough only shrugged, chewing complacently on his stogie.

'I'd rather have me a mule than a woman any day.'

Firmly the wagonmaster resettled his sombrero and turning, lifted one hand over his head in a gesture of command. 'Get set to move out!'

'Birdie—' Leah came swiftly to the woman's side, then impulsively bent a kiss on the leathery cheek. The ghost of a smile crossed her lips. 'You've caught yourself a fine man, Birdie Gordon.'

'Child,' Birdie's voice held a hushed pity, 'I'm sorry, mighty sorry, 'bout what happened. It don't seem fair, you losing yer man, jest when you found him—'

'No! Birdie—no!' Fiercely Leah interrupted her. 'No, you mustn't say that! All this week I've felt so lost—so empty—I didn't want to go on. But I was wrong and Mr Simms is right! Cole's sacrifice can't be in vain. I've got to take courage from his memory, I've got to go on, on to California, I've got to find a dream for both of us . . .'

In the new thinness of her face, Leah's eyes were enormous, a great green blaze lit by an inner spirit that went past the pain moving in their depths. 'I—I once told Cole that love was stronger than hate.' She paused, then went softly, surely on. 'I know now it's stronger even than death. We can never—really—be parted.'

'Wagons ho!'

From the saddle of the big bay, came Alonzo Simms' order to move out, to move ahead, into the Promised Land. Head high in determination, Leah nodded at Birdie, urging her forward, to the wagon. Faltering only slightly, she followed.

And then suddenly she stopped. Her heart leapt and checked and began racing. For breaking over the slow creaking of wagon wheels was the roll of hoofbeats.

As if rent with sudden pain, she clutched a slender hand to the base of her throat, the horrible fear pulsing within that the sound was but in her imagination. But no—no—! The pounding rhythm sang ever louder— ever nearer.

Leah spun around and began running. The shawl slipped from her head, her hair streaming out behind her, arms outstretched. Wildly, Cole spurred his mount on, then abruptly, he reined in, watching her come towards him, looking at her as if he'd never have enough of looking.

There was a crude bandage swathed about his forehead, and his dark face—bearded, creased with the grit of the trail, seared with fatigue—was the face she had first seen in the darkness of night.

But now the tawny gaze held new peace. And now it was in the fullness of morning sunlight that she took the last steps towards him.

He leaned down in the saddle and stretched out a hand to her, and as she answered his touch, a flame leapt in his eyes, an answering light in her own. Leah knew they needed no words to seal their promise. Never had they needed words. From the first moment her heart had beat as one with this man's.

He swung her into the saddle before him, his arms going around her, and at his nearness—as always and forever—her own body quickened. This, too, Leah knew was the way it must always be between them—this need, this want, this insistence.

At the touch of light spurs, the horse moved forward, carrying them both towards the golden valley below.